EARLY

"Tasche Laine's *CHAMELEON* hooked me at the beginning!... If you want a great plot, caring mother, and thrilling tale of how Tara becomes Geoffrey's prey, you will enjoy this book."

—Brandi's Consulting, *Book Blogger*

"Tasche Laine couldn't have picked a better title than *CHAMELEON* for her new mind-twisting psychological thriller. It sucked me in from the beginning...the sharp plot twists kept me intrigued till the end."

—*Heidi Lynn's Book Reviews*

"A terrific follow-up to *CLOSURE,* which I enjoyed immensely. *CHAMELEON* is richly packed with engaging characters and plot turns that keep you moving through the story.... Great story line and believable characters. A definite good read you don't want to miss!"

—Scott B. Allan, *Book Reviewer*

"Fast-paced and exhilarating.... Tara meets a man who plays mind games with her, and she can't help but be who he wants her to be. The story is suspenseful to the end."

—NB, *Goodreads*

"A great writer indeed! I was captivated from the beginning!"

—Brenda

"The author did a great job managing the intricacies of a relationship with someone so psychologically...challenged. Chameleon is the perfect name for the book—once you read it, you'll know why too!"

—Jordin

CHAMELEON

CHAMELEON

TASCHE LAINE

CHAMELEON. Copyright © 2019 by Tasche Laine.
All rights reserved.
Cover photo by Engin Akyurt.

ISBN-13: 978-1-7321261-3-8 (eBook)
ISBN-13: 978-1-7321261-4-5 (pbk.)

Skye Blue Press
Vancouver, WA

For Glenn, Izzy, Jack Henry, and Buck
in memory of
our beloved Dorey.
When I think of you, which is often,
I know a piece of Dorey lives on.
She remains indelibly in my heart for eternity.

And just to be clear… F*ck Cancer.

Prologue

JEFF JENSEN SAT in the back of the police car, hands cuffed behind his back. He heard Rayna and Riki pleading, "Please don't take away our daddy! Pleeeease!" The six-year-old identical twin girls resembled their blue-eyed, blonde-haired mother, and looked nothing like Jeff.

Jeff had married their mom a year ago and she'd insisted her kids call him Daddy. All three of them.

He stared out the back of the squad car at the scene of the twins crying and clinging to their mom's legs, his wife ignoring them and talking to a cop, his stepson talking to a lady in a suit—*probably a shrink or social worker*. He wondered how he'd ended up in this mess.

"Ma'am?" Officer Dave Reynolds rubbed his furrowed brow and glanced over at Jeff through the window. He was wearing a wife-beater and Reynolds spotted a tattoo of a samurai sword on his shoulder. The smug look on his face was unnerving. "Are you sure you don't want me to take this guy in and charge him? These are pretty serious allegations by your son, and—"

"Yes, I'm sure. Brayden lied," the frazzled woman said while biting her lip. "I'm sorry, Officer. It won't happen again. My son got upset because Jeff told him to do his homework. That's all. He's just trying to get out of it. Believe me, he has no idea what he's done. Check him yourself. There are no marks on him. He made the whole thing up."

Reynolds clenched his jaw and leveled his gaze at her. "As a matter of fact, the child psychologist is with your son now. We'll see what—"

"Let it go, Reynolds," Sergeant Murphy interrupted. "Her story checks out. The boy admitted he made it all up. You can release Mr. Jensen. We're dropping the charges."

Reynolds heaved a sigh. He walked over and yanked Jeff out of the squad car. "Looks like it's yer lucky night, buddy."

Right before he unlocked the handcuffs, Reynolds leaned over and whispered in Jeff's ear, "But don't get too comfortable. I'm watching you."

His soft gray eyes locked with Jeff's menacing brown eyes for a beat. He saw a darkness behind them that made his skin crawl.

The 38-year-old cop broke the stare and unlocked the cuffs.

Jeff smiled.

"I understand, Officer. No hard feelings. Have a nice night." He winked at Reynolds as he rubbed his newly freed wrists.

With his wife and stepchildren obediently trailing after him, Jeff Jensen walked back toward his 3,800-square-foot home in Newport Beach, California—a free man.

Despite the occasional call to 9-1-1 by his obnoxious ten-year-old stepson Brayden, Jeff had a decent life. He was a successful business executive, in excellent physical condition, and strikingly handsome—at least that's what everyone told him. Being half Japanese and half Danish gave him a slightly exotic look, and chicks seemed to dig it.

He lived on the beach in an upscale neighborhood and seemed to have it all. But Sheila, his wife, was more trouble than she was worth. How he got roped into marriage and three stepkids was the handiwork of the five-foot-eleven stunner who entranced him with her seductive ways.

With long, silky, blonde curls, sun-kissed tan, and an enormous fake rack (that he'd paid for), she was the stuff of teenage boys' wet dreams. But no chick was worth the trouble she put him through because of that stupid brat kid and his psycho dad, Sheila's ex.

And that damn cop. What was his name? *Reynolds.* Yes, Reynolds. He had to shake Reynolds off his tail. He couldn't risk that nosy cop poking around in his business. He couldn't risk anyone finding out about his past, especially a nosy cop. Not now, with so much to lose.

Hell, not ever, if I can help it. It's settled. I'll leave tonight.

It took two years of hard work, but Geoffrey Jensen had created a whole new life for himself. He was now a licensed Marriage and Family Therapist (MFT) with his own practice. He had decided the name 'Geoffrey' was more professional than 'Jeff,' so he changed it. Besides, he liked the idea of starting over with a new name for his new life.

He had a way with people and believed he was a good listener. He also presumed to make a lot of money listening to people's problems. Becoming a therapist sounded like the perfect solution. He had hated his job as the VP of sales for Broadchem Corporation. He wanted a fresh start.

He had graduated from Chapman University's Marriage and Family Therapy Master of Arts program and had been assured a very lucrative career; one he couldn't wait to get started.

He'd walked away from his business, his home, and his marriage. He'd walked out on his life.

After selling his house for a tidy sum of $2.4 million and paying off the lawyers and ex-wife, he'd still had more than enough for his graduate studies. He had walked away with $650,000.

Living off his savings and renting a small apartment in Costa Mesa, he had attended classes full-time. He planned to make the money back easily once he got his new practice going. But clients didn't just walk in and line his pockets with cash; he would have to hustle to gain a clientele.

Geoffrey Jensen had a plan for his new life; one where he could hide in plain sight.

1

Tara

SINGLE MOTHER TARA Spencer immersed herself into her daughter's life. She actively volunteered at Jalina's school, belonged to the PTA, and dedicated countless volunteer hours to the sixth grader's many musical theater productions. Jalina loved musical theater and rehearsals were currently underway with her children's community theater group for *Beauty and the Beast,* in which she had the lead part. This was her dream role because Belle was her favorite Disney princess.

Tara devoted all her spare time to Jalina and was relieved the eleven-year-old was well adjusted and happy, despite having divorced parents and shuttling back and forth between two households. Since the demise of her fourteen years with Joe, Jalina's dad, and the failed attempt at getting back together with her first love, Trey, dating was the last thing on Tara's mind. She happily welcomed the distractions that came with being a single parent.

When Tara's divorce had become final in May, she and Jalina had rented a cozy three-bedroom condo in Tustin. It was close enough to Joe, who was still at the Fullerton house, to allow them to share custody of Jalina. Since her new job with a TV series filmed in Newport Beach she had moved to Tustin to minimize the commute.

It was the first time she had lived without a man since President Bill Clinton was in office, *Braveheart* was number one at the box office, and Michael Jordan came out of retirement. Now that it was November 2, 2009, Tara felt occasional loneliness.

The divorce had been a civil and amicable one, as she had reminded herself that Joe was the father of her daughter. She hadn't wanted to drag him through a lengthy court battle. Why get lawyers involved when they could just dissolve the marriage peacefully themselves?

They had agreed to an even fifty-fifty joint custody, which meant she had Jalina every other week. Joe still traveled often for his job as a sales manager for a local toy company, which was great for Tara because she got Jalina even more. Unfortunately for Jalina, it meant a few disappointments when her dad couldn't make it to certain school events.

"Mom! I got the solo in our fall concert!" Jalina shouted, while slamming the car door shut when Tara picked her up from school.

"That's great sweetie, but don't slam the door."

"Sorry," she winced. "Um, do you think Daddy will be there?"

"When is the concert again?"

"It's Thursday."

"I'm sorry sweetie, but I think your dad has a business trip—"

"Nooo! It's not fair! Why doesn't he get to come to any of my shows?"

"I know you're disappointed, honey. I'll record it on video for him and we can send it—"

"It's not the same!"

"True, but at least he'll still get to see it."

"Why does he have to travel all the time? It's not fair! Doesn't he want to see me?"

"Honey, of course he wants to see you. Don't you ever think that Daddy doesn't want to see you. He just has a very demanding job and part of that job requires that he go out of town a lot."

"Daddy says he has to pay you money. Is that why he has to work so hard? Why he leaves all the time, so he can make more money? So he can afford to pay you?" Jalina hesitated for a second, then screamed, "It's your fault he can't come to my concert!"

Tara knew she had to choose her next words very carefully. Getting defensive and setting the record straight would only make things worse. Joe's income was substantially more than Tara's but Jalina was just a kid and didn't need to understand the nuances of child support. Besides, that wasn't the issue here. Jalina loved her father and was hurt that he would miss another event. She just needed a way to vent her frustration.

Tara took a deep breath, "Jalina, sweetie, I know you don't mean that. I'll tell your dad about the concert and if there is any way he can be there you know he will. We both love you very much."

They sat in silence the rest of the ride home.

"Jalina hates me," Tara complained to her friend, Dorey, later that night.

"Oh, please! That kid fuckin' adores you. She's just going

through a rough patch, that's all. Now cheer up and pass me the damn wine," Dorey smirked with a twinkle in her dancing fern-green eyes.

At five-foot-nine, fit and muscular from years of playing tennis, thirty-four-year old Dorey Dalton was a feisty redhead and a force to be reckoned with. An Executive Lifestyle Concierge for Marriott International, Dorey traveled extensively so it was a rare Monday night that she was in town. Tara soaked up all the 'Dorey time' she could get with her neighbor and new friend.

"You always put things in perspective for me, Dorey. Thanks. I needed some of your wisdom," Tara smiled at her.

"*My* wisdom? 'We are here to laugh at the odds and live our lives so well that death will tremble to take us.' Bukowski said that. Now that's some wisdom." Dorey adjusted her seat cushion as the two women sat on Tara's patio that balmy evening sharing a bottle of Chardonnay and discussing Tara's problems. "Tara, you know what you need?"

"I can't imagine. No, what do I need?"

"Lady, you need to get laid!"

"Really? And just how do you suggest I do that?"

"Funny you should ask," Dorey said, as she poured more wine. "I just met the perfect guy for you and he gave me his number. He is HOT! We're talkin' major eye candy with muscles upon muscles. Oh, and he's a psychologist."

"What? You're serious?" Tara was incredulous. "No way. I'm not ready and I don't need to be analyzed. After the divorce and then things not working out with Trey...I just don't trust my judgment in men anymore."

"Wait, who's Trey? You dated after your divorce from Joe? Before you met me?"

"Yeah, I told you. Trey was my childhood sweetheart.

We broke up when we were nineteen. We kept in touch a little over the years but we both married other people and I always wondered what it would have been like for us if we'd stayed together. I guess you could say I never really got over him. He was my first love.

"Anyway, after Joe filed for divorce, I looked up Trey and he was single but living in Phoenix. We emailed and called each other for a month then finally set up a face-to-face. It had been twenty years since we'd last seen each other."

"Oh yeah, I remember now. Then you tried dating and the long-distance relationship thing for a few months but it didn't work out. Right?"

"Right. He wasn't the same person I'd fallen in love with when we were fifteen. But, who is? I realized we weren't meant to be together, ended it once and for all, and finally got my closure.

"When my divorce with Joe became finalized five months ago, I moved here and met you. As you can see, I don't need another complication in my life right now."

"Christ sakes, ya don't have to marry the guy. Just meet him, go on a few dates, screw his brains out and have a good time."

"I don't think so. I mean, I don't casually—"

"Tara, you deserve to have some fun. Don't get me wrong, Jalina's a great kid and I love her to death but she's not gonna scratch your itch, ya know? Stop being such a Mommy and do something for yourself for once."

"If he's so hot what will he see in me?"

"Are you kidding me? Lady, you're gorgeous! With those Carolina blue eyes and cute little figure you got goin' on, he'd be nuts not to be into you. And I love your thick brown hair."

"Stop, you're making me blush," Tara playfully hit

Dorey's arm. "But you're obviously delusional. Your red hair is to die for. I love those locks, like an unruly lion's mane."

"Thanks. Don't change the subject."

"You're not going to let this go, are you?"

"Nope!"

"Great," Tara sighed. "All right, who is this guy? How did you meet him and what's his name?"

"Speed dating!"

"WHAT—?"

"Hey, watch it, Miss Judgy Pants. When you've been single as long as I have, let's see how well you meet men."

"But you work for Marriott. You travel all over the world and meet tons of people every day—"

"True, but it's not like you think. Most of the men I meet are either married, gay, or too old. Besides, I don't interact with the hotel guests much and we're not allowed to date them. Do you want me to tell you about this guy or not?"

"Okay, but why don't you want to date him?"

"He's too old for me," Dorey laughed. "But he's perfect for you, only a year older, I think. Forty-four?"

"Great, now you're calling me old?"

"No way, lady. I didn't say that. I just like them really young, that's all."

Dorey gave her a wink and finished off the last of the wine.

The next evening just after Tara tucked Jalina in for the night at nine-thirty she received a text from a phone number she didn't recognize. She compared the number on her cell phone's screen to the number Dorey gave her the night before. It was a match.

"Darn it Dorey! You knew I'd never call him so you

took the liberty to intercede on my behalf, huh?" she said out loud to an empty living room.

Upon hearing Tara's voice, Nala jumped up on the brown leather couch and onto her lap, licking her face with the excitement of a new puppy. The seventy-pound red Goldendoodle had been with Tara since May. She recalled the night her co-worker, Jackie, dropped off the dog. It was the same day she had received the divorce papers in the mail declaring her divorce resolved. It was a bittersweet moment.

Jackie was the 2nd Assistant Director (A.D.) on *The Bad Wife*, a new TV series where she and Tara worked together. One of Jackie's duties was to oversee the movements of the cast, ensuring the principal actors were in makeup, in wardrobe, or standing by on the set at the correct times. She was Tara's main point of contact for the kids.

Tara's job as the set tutor, is called a Studio Teacher. She tutored the two child actors on the show. She ensured they met their state mandated three hours of schooling each day.

Jackie got an offer to be a 1st A.D. on a movie trilogy filming in Moorea, French Polynesia, in the South Pacific. For her it was the opportunity and location destination of a lifetime and she couldn't pass it up. But sadly it also meant she couldn't take her sweet dog, Nala.

Jackie made Tara promise two things when she gave Nala to her that night, "First, don't change her name. She is Nala, named after Nala of *The Lion King*, which means 'successful.' I believe she is my good luck charm and now I'm passing my sweet good luck charm onto you; may you enjoy her and the joy she brings you as much as I have. I am truly blessed.

"Second," Jackie continued. "Don't treat her like a dog. She is family and my best friend. I have taken her everywhere with me for the last two years and she hates being alone. She loves everyone and has never met a person she didn't like. Take good care of her for me, okay?"

Tara smiled at the memory, looked into Nala's soft, trusting brown eyes and scratched just behind her ears. "You're a sweet girl, Nala. I'm so glad we found each other. Are you my good luck charm now?" She sighed, looked over at her phone, and picked it up to read the text.

"Hi Tara! Dorey told me about you. She sent me a picture and gave me your number. I hope it's okay that I'm contacting you. I would like to get to know you better...can I call you some time? By the way, you have a beautiful smile! :)

I hope to hear from you soon,
Geoffrey"

After reading the text, Tara tossed the cell phone back down onto the couch unsure if she wanted to reply. She heard the familiar ping again. This time it included a photo of Geoffrey. It showed him from the waist up wearing a dark gray athletic tank top. He had short black hair, almond eyes, high cheekbones, strong jaw, kissably full lips, straight white teeth, and bulging biceps. It was obvious he worked out.

Wow. Perhaps I'm being too hasty...maybe I should give this guy a chance. I mean, what could it hurt, right? She thought these words silently this time, not wanting to disturb Nala, sleeping peacefully and resting her head on Tara's lap.

Snatching up her phone again, she typed out a reply with her index finger. Since texting was new for her she hadn't quite mastered using her thumbs as she'd seen teenagers do.

"Hi Geoffrey. Nice to 'meet' you," Tara replied. "I'd like to get to know you better as well. Thanks for the compliment. By the way, you're not so bad yourself. ;)"

Just then, the phone rang in her hand and she nearly dropped it, startling her and waking up Nala. It was Geoffrey. *Man, this guy doesn't waste any time.* "Hello?" she half whispered, trying to find her voice.

"Hello, Tara. It's Geoffrey. How are you?"

"I'm good…how about you?"

"Great. I'm so glad you took my call. Dorey said wonderful things about you and I can't wait to meet you."

"Sorry, you have me at a disadvantage. She didn't tell me much about you."

"Well, yeah, that's because we hardly know each other," he laughed.

They talked for nearly an hour. By the time Tara hung up, she'd agreed to meet him Friday night at BJ's Restaurant at seven o'clock.

A mixture of fear, nerves, dread and excitement all rolled into a tight ball of tension she wondered if this was a good idea.

2

They Meet

IT WAS FRIDAY night. Tara rushed home from work, made sure Jalina and Nala had everything they needed for their sleepover at Jalina's best friend Skyler's house and changed clothes for her date with Geoffrey. She settled on a casual look of jeans and a long-sleeved gray striped t-shirt.

A bundle of nerves and pressed for time, Tara despised being late. "Jalina! Come on, let's go. I need to drop you off on my way," she called up the stairs while checking her watch for the third time.

"Oooh, Mommy, you look beautiful," Jalina gushed as she and Nala came bounding down the stairs. Her concert had been the night before. Joe had made it there in time and Jalina received a standing ovation for her performance.

She had an amazing voice, especially for only being eleven. The kid was a natural and neither Joe nor Tara knew who she got her pipes from because no one else in the family could sing. At least not well.

"All set?"

"Yep."

"Okay, grab Nala's leash and let's go."

Tara showed up at BJ's three minutes early. Just as she parked her car, Geoffrey called to let her know he was nearly there. She went inside and sat down in the lobby area scanning the restaurant's contemporary décor. Consisting of hardwood floors, warm earth tones and brick walls, it had a sports bar relaxed atmosphere with a few big screen TV's in the bar.

A few minutes later, Geoffrey walked in and easily spotted Tara. He locked eyes with her and strode across the lobby stopping an inch in front of her. *'Wow'* was all she could think as she stood up and greeted him with a nervous grin.

"Hey, Tara. It's so nice to finally meet you," he smiled broadly and gave her a brief hug.

'Finally' meet me? It's only been three days, Tara thought, thrown by his greeting. She managed a "Yeah, you, too," in reply, still lost in her thoughts.

"I can take you to your table now," the hostess said.

Tara followed her to a table near the kitchen and noticed her own sweaty palms. She wiped them on the front of her jeans also noting that Dorey hadn't exaggerated when she'd described Geoffrey as 'hot.' He wore designer jeans, fitted navy button-up shirt, untucked with the cuffs turned up and black loafers. He looked even better in person than in his picture.

Tara stopped short when she heard Geoffrey ask, "Do you have a booth in a quieter area? I want to be able to converse with this lovely lady without distractions."

"Certainly, sir, right this way." The hostess led them to a booth in a quiet corner. "Your server will be with you shortly. May I get you two started with a drink?"

Geoffrey looked at Tara and saw her hesitate so he ordered, "Ice tea for me," and waited.

"I'll have ice tea, too, please," Tara blushed.

When the hostess left Geoffrey turned his attention to Tara. "So, Tara, Dorey tells me you're a Studio Teacher? What does that entail?"

"Um, I tutor kids in the entertainment industry. I mean, not acting lessons...I'm the teacher on set for the required schooling of minors who work in the industry."

"The industry?"

"Yes, the 'industry' as it relates to entertainment, in Hollywood and elsewhere. Any time a child performer is compensated, such as a child model or actor for photo shoots, film, TV and on stage, a Studio Teacher is required. Meaning, the working children go to school on set for three hours a day and I'm their teacher for the day. I'm also responsible for their health, safety and welfare while they're on set. I'm their advocate and enforce the child labor laws."

"So, they get credit for going to school while working on a movie?"

"Yes, if it's a multi-day project I'm in touch with their classroom teachers, and sometimes school principal to make sure they get all their assignments, quizzes and tests, and don't fall behind. They get the same workload they'd get if they physically attended their own school."

"That sounds very interesting. I bet you meet a lot of celebrities?"

"Yeah, I do," she fingered the aquamarine ring on the middle finger of her left hand looking uncomfortable. It was just a reminder that her ring finger was bare. Clearing her throat, she continued, "Geoffrey, I need to tell you something."

"Of course, you can tell me anything. What is it?" he encouraged.

"I'm nervous. I mean laughable, butterflies, high school nervous. I feel like an idiot."

"It's okay, Tara. There's nothing to feel nervous about." His voice was soft, soothing. "Just take a deep calming breath. In…and out. Good. Again, inhale and think only about your breathing. Then, exhale very slowly. Feel your body begin to relax as you exhale. Good."

She did as he instructed and began to calm down. His voice was deep and hypnotic and she soon felt relaxed and comfortable. She was relieved he didn't laugh at her and asked him how he knew to calm her down like that.

"Easy. I'm a psychotherapist. Helping people feel better is what I do."

"But Dorey told me you were a psychologist. Are they the same thing?"

"Not exactly. A psychologist can be a psychotherapist, but not the other way around. To be a therapist or counselor, a Master's degree is required. And to be a psychologist a doctorate degree is required."

"Wow. You have a PhD?"

"No. A PhD is a Doctor of Philosophy. A Doctor of Psychology is a PsyD."

"Do people call you Dr. Jensen?"

"Sometimes," he chuckled. "But I ask my patients to call me Geoffrey. I find the informal tone makes them more comfortable."

"Oh," Tara took it in, nodding.

"As I was about to tell you, I also practice mindfulness which I think would be good for you. It is essentially a form of meditation where you achieve a mental state by focusing your awareness on the present moment. When you are aware of being in the present you can then calmly acknowledge and accept your feelings, thoughts, and bodily sensations. Once you acknowledge them you have the ability to control and change them."

Tara was fascinated by Geoffrey's every word; bewitched as if under his spell. Transfixed by the sound of his voice, she happily listened to him talk about why he got into therapy, his ex-wife and step-kids, and walking away from a high-powered executive job where he made half a million dollars a year.

He regaled her with funny stories about his doctoral degree program, life as a full-time grad student in his 40s, and how he easily paid his tuition in full. He said he graduated from grad school with a doctorate to add to his two Master's degrees (the first was in business) and zero debt.

He told her he left the rat race to pursue a more altruistic and meaningful career. He said there were people out there who were hurting and needed to be helped and he wanted to help them. Tara soaked up every word, completely unaware that Geoffrey did the majority of the talking for the duration of the evening.

They ended up closing the place down and had spent five hours together which seemed unusual to Tara considering it was the first time they'd ever met. Yet, she felt at ease with Geoffrey, as though they'd known each other for years. The connection was instant. He was very attentive and said all the right things. So far, it was the perfect first date.

"Thank you again for dinner tonight, Geoffrey," Tara said as they walked out. "I'm really glad you called. To be honest, I'm not sure I would have called you. Thank goodness Dorey took matters into her own hands and called you herself."

"Funny you should mention that. I love how Dorey took

charge and made it happen. She's very proactive and I like proactive women. The last woman I dated before you was a doctor, before that I dated a lawyer. I've actually never dated a teacher before. I'm used to strong, assertive women who know what they want. Tara, do you know what you want?"

"Well, I know that I want to see you again."

"Good answer," he smiled. He opened her car door for her, hugged her, and said good night.

As Tara got into her car and drove home she wondered if she had what it would take to be the confident, assertive woman Geoffrey said he wanted.

3

First Kiss

THE NEXT MORNING, Geoffrey sent Tara a text with "xo" at the end.

"Did you just kiss me?" she texted back.

"Yes, I believe I did! Now we've gotten that first kiss out of the way!"

"Indeed. LOL. Speaking of first kisses…how old were you the first time you kissed a girl?"

"12. She kissed me. She pinned me up against the locker in the hallway at school and made her move. Like I said, most of the girls in my life have been the assertive ones. Both of my ex-wives proposed to me."

"Both? I thought you'd only been married once?"

"Ah. That's a conversation for another time. How about I pick you up at 6 tonight and tell you about it?"

"Sounds great. I'll text you my address now. See you soon." Tara sent the texts along with her address and couldn't wait to tell Dorey all about last night. But it would have to wait because Dorey was out of town on business.

Tara drove to Skyler McKeever's house to pick up Jalina and Nala from their sleepover. When she got there Jalina begged to spend one more night. "Please! We're having so much fun!"

The two girls attended the same school and were in *Beauty and the Beast* together. Since they both had leading roles, Skyler was Mrs. Potts and Jalina was Belle, they had the same rehearsal schedule. Skyler's mom, Nicolee, was a stay-home mom and often drove the girls to play rehearsals or school events when Tara couldn't. Plus, they'd been best friends since first grade. Tara and Jalina both adored Skyler's family.

But Tara was torn. She enjoyed spending her days off with her daughter and next week was Joe's turn to have Jalina. Yet she had a date planned with Geoffrey that night and it was way too soon for them to meet. It would only be their second date.

"What about play rehearsal?"

"Skyler's mom can take me. But, can you take Nala home? She only likes it over here if I'm with her the whole time and we'll be gone for a while."

"But I haven't said yes yet," Tara frowned.

"Please? All my homework is done, my room is clean, and Skyler really wants me to stay."

"I see. How could I argue with that logic?" Tara winked.

"Yay! Thank you, Mommy!"

"Wait. I need to make sure it's cool with Nicolee first," Tara walked into the kitchen and found Nicolee loading the dishwasher. "Hey, Nicolee."

"Hi, Tara. Good to see you."

"You, too. So, the girls haven't driven you crazy yet? Are you sure it's okay if Jalina stays another night?"

"Of course. We love having her and it's no trouble at all. Actually, Jalina keeps Skyler out of my hair so you could say you're doing me a favor by loaning her out."

"Okay," Tara laughed. "Thanks for having her over. See you tomorrow." She walked to the stairs, "Jalina, come give me a hug."

Jalina, Skyler, and Nala raced down the stairs. "Thank you, Mommy!" Jalina tackled Tara as she jumped into the air, wrapping her arms and legs around her.

"You're welcome, sweetie. Be good. I love you."

"I love you, too. Bye." The girls giggled with excitement and went back upstairs. Tara waved to Skyler's parents and let herself out the door.

"Come on, Nala. Let's go home."

At exactly six o'clock Tara heard a knock on the door. She rushed outside and closed the door behind her before Nala could start barking. Geoffrey stood on her front porch in a black button-up shirt, dark jeans, and two red roses in his hand. "Two roses to commemorate our second date," he said.

"Thank you, Geoffrey. That's so sweet." Tara took the roses from him, putting them up to her nose to take in their sweetly fragrant scent. "Actually, roses are my favorite flower. I know it seems cliché but I think they're beautiful."

They stood outside long enough to make it awkward when Tara said, "Sorry, where are my manners? Please come in and I'll go get a vase."

"Thanks." Geoffrey gave Tara a quick side hug, stepped inside, and strolled toward the living room. "Nice place you have here. Do you own it?"

"No, it's a rental," Tara called from the kitchen already filling a vase with water. "I've only lived here a few months. I haven't even organized the spare room yet; it's still filled with boxes."

Just then, Nala barked three times and ran toward Geoffrey. "Hey, who's this? You didn't tell me you had a dog." Nala sniffed his hand but flinched when he tried to pet her. "What's the deal? Is your dog skittish?"

Tara walked out of the kitchen and set the roses on the dining table. "Actually, no." She patted Nala on the head and they watched her walk over to her water dish, tail down. "She's usually very friendly. In fact, you're lucky she didn't jump up on you. I've only had her a few months and have been trying to get her to stop jumping up on people."

"Well, it looks like it's working," he glanced at the dog, completely ignoring them now. "You look beautiful, by the way. The blue in your sundress matches your eyes perfectly."

"Thank you," Tara blushed. "Would you like a quick tour of my place?"

"No time. I don't want to be late for our reservation," Geoffrey glanced at his watch.

"Okay then. I'm ready. Shall we go?"

"Absolutely. Oh, I parked out front so we could leave right away."

"Good thing no one noticed."

"Why?"

"Because you're parked in front of a fire hydrant."

"Yeah, well, I knew I'd be right back. Besides, it's not likely I'd get a parking ticket in a residential area."

Tara raised her eyebrows at this, "You'd be surprised."

"Well then, let's get out of here," Geoffrey chuckled. He opened the passenger door to his black Acura NSX.

"This is a nice car," Tara complimented, as she ran her hand across the plush black leather then reached over and buckled her seat belt.

"It's all right. Actually, I've been thinking about getting a newer model. This one's already two years old."

At Rodrigo's Mexican Grill, Geoffrey ordered fish tacos for both of them which Tara thought was odd because he said he preferred assertive women. *Yet, I'm not allowed to order my own food?*

Tara had a mojito with dinner and Geoffrey stuck with water citing he didn't drink because it wasn't healthy. He worked out five days a week and only ate healthy food.

"I wish I had your discipline. I haven't worked out in a while and I definitely need to eat better. My weaknesses are ice cream and nachos. But not together." Tara laughed to a silent Geoffrey and realized her joke fell flat.

Feeling self-conscious, she wished she hadn't brought it up. Her bad eating habits had caused fifteen pounds of weight gain since the divorce. Probably more, but she didn't want to weigh herself to find out. She absent-mindedly twirled the ring on her middle finger with her thumb.

"You're nervous, aren't you?" Geoffrey mused.

"How did you know?"

"You have a tell. Everyone does. Some people are more mindful about their actions and better at covering up, that's all."

"Oh? What's my tell?"

"You fidget with your ring."

"Do I? Hmm…I think that might have to do with more than just my being nervous…. You see, I miss wearing a ring on my ring finger. After so many years of wearing one, it feels naked now. Is that silly?"

"Not at all. I completely understand."

"Oh, good. I thought wearing a ring on my left hand would help, but it doesn't."

"I can train you if you want."

"Excuse me?"

"You mentioned you want to work out more, get in shape. I used to be a fitness model and I've also done some personal training on the side. I have blackbelts in Karate and Aikido, and I've been working out since I was thirteen."

"Impressive." Tara, now slightly intimidated, tried not to show it by remaining casual. "What's Aikido?"

"It's a Japanese martial art that means 'the way of the spirit of harmony.' It's not as forceful as Karate, but it does employ the use of Japanese weapons such as the sword, staff and knife. I have a samurai sword, called a katana, that used to belong to my grandfather and his grandfather before him. In fact, it's been in my family for many generations. I had it appraised once and it's believed to be at least 400 years old."

"Wow. That's so cool that your family has been able to preserve a part of their past like that and that the sword has been passed down all those generations. Do you think your ancestors were Samurai warriors?"

"Yes, I do. I've read a lot about the feudal area of Japan. It's quite fascinating. Would you like to see my katana sometime?"

"Yes, I'd like that."

The waitress appeared at their table, "How is everything? Another mojito?"

"Everything is fine, thank you. Tara? Are you going to have another drink?" Geoffrey asked.

"No, thank you. Just some more water, please." Tara wondered if Geoffrey judged her for having a drink at all. His tone seemed almost stern.

"Certainly, I'll be right back." The waitress left and came back immediately with a pitcher of water.

When she left the second time, Tara asked the question

that had been bothering her all day. "You mentioned earlier today that you've been married twice? What happened with your first marriage?"

Geoffrey sighed. "Ah, I wondered if you'd bring that up. Nothing much to talk about, really. My first wife and I met when we were very young. We were both modeling and met through the agency. She was all about her career. She left me after two years to chase her dreams in Europe. She was on her way to becoming an international fashion model and rise to superstardom."

"Wow. What's her name? Have I heard of her?"

"Sadly, no. When she got to Europe she ruined her life with a cocaine addiction. She never became famous and I lost track of her years ago. Haven't thought of her since, until now. Aren't you the curious one?"

"What? I'm just trying to get to know you better. I'm curious about you. She's a part of your history, and I want to—"

"I don't like to talk about it." Geoffrey leaned forward and locked eyes with Tara. "You know, it's not healthy to talk about exes or past relationships. People who are stuck in the past aren't able to enjoy their present. It's in the past; we should   focus on the here and now. Mindfulness, remember? And right now, I want to focus on the beautiful woman sitting across from me."

When Geoffrey took Tara home, she invited him in. Nala didn't run to see her at the door like she usually did and Tara worried that she might be sick. "Please make yourself at home, Geoffrey. I'm just going to take Nala out for a quick walk."

When they got back, Nala skulked over to her dog bed in the corner of the living room and laid down completely ignoring Geoffrey. *That's so odd,* Tara thought, but she decided not to say anything yet. She didn't want to hurt Geoffrey's feelings but she was pretty sure her dog didn't like him.

They sat on the couch and talked until two in the morning. He told her more about his profession, psychotherapy, mindfulness and meditation.

Tara was interested in what he had to say and his voice took on a dreamy, hypnotic quality. But she was so distracted by his mouth she could barely control herself. She'd never been so drawn to a man's lips before. His were full and supple. *And those perfectly straight, white teeth, and radiant smile…what would it be like to kiss him?*

She noticed he hadn't made a move toward her yet and frowned. *Don't most guys make a move by now? He said all his exes kissed him first. He said he likes assertive women. Oh my gosh, this isn't me. What's my problem? I sound obsessed.*

With a sigh, Tara cleared her throat. "Geoffrey?" she paused. "Sorry to interrupt you but I have a confession to make."

"Oh?"

"Uh, yeah, this is kind of embarrassing to admit but I've been trying to come up with a clever line about our text kisses and was wondering about a real kiss."

"You didn't ask."

"Do I need to ask?"

"Isn't that what you're doing now?"

Tara blushed and gave a slight nod.

"I can do that," he smiled.

Geoffrey leaned in and put his hand on Tara's face. He pressed his lips to hers then parted them as he kissed her. It was warm, wet and soft.

He sat back and asked, "How was that?"

"Good," she grinned. She hugged him and he rubbed her back while they held each other.

He kissed her again. This time, it was more passionate, probing. This time, he kissed her like he meant it.

Tara broke away slightly breathless. While she was trying to collect her thoughts, Geoffrey blurted out, "Tara, what do you want in a relationship? What are you looking for?"

"Wow, that came out of nowhere," she laughed.

Geoffrey was unfazed. His fixed gaze almost unnerved her. "Oh, you're serious. Okay, well…I know I don't want to repeat the mistakes I made in my marriage. I hope I learned from that and will be a better partner in my next relationship."

She took a drink of water and continued, "Basically, I want what everyone wants—to love and be loved. When I'm ready, I'll want a partner to share my life with. I need someone I can trust, who communicates well, has integrity, and a great sense of humor. I'm sure I'll think of more later. I just wasn't prepared for the question. What do you want?"

"I don't want to be somebody's second or third priority. People shouldn't put their kids first above their mate. I want someone who is available to spend time with me."

"I see." Tara couldn't look at him just then. *I guess I better not dare talk about Jalina too much. He doesn't get it. He's not a parent.*

4

Chameleon

SUNDAY MORNING TARA slept in due to her late-night talk with Geoffrey the night before. She took a quick shower, dried her hair, and got dressed. She didn't want to be late picking up Jalina from youth group. When the girls spent Saturday nights together, whether at Tara's house or Nicolee's, the moms had an arrangement to meet in the church parking lot the next day. There, they exchanged kids and their overnight bags from each other.

Since becoming a Christian nine years earlier, Tara went to church off and on but struggled with her new faith and still considered herself a fledgling.

Last night Geoffrey told her, "I subscribe to the teachings of Buddha but I don't believe there's a God."

Tara didn't know anything about Buddhism so she decided to keep an open mind. But as she parked in the church parking lot to get Jalina, she felt guilty and wondered if Geoffrey was right for her. She decided to talk to Dorey about it.

That evening, after dropping Jalina and Nala off for their week at Joe's, Tara went over to Dorey's place. Dorey lived two doors down from Tara. She knocked on the door and waited, hoping Dorey was in town from her latest business trip.

"Hey, pretty lady, good to see ya," Dorey grinned as she gave Tara a big bear hug.

"You, too," Tara entered the cluttered, eclectic condo and cleared a spot to sit on the couch. "How was your trip?"

"Fabulous. I love my job." Dorey went in the kitchen to get some wine. "Last week the Amalfi Coast in Italy, next week Montreal. Good thing I love to travel. But don't think for a minute you're gonna get me talking about myself right now. Was your date with Geoffrey incredible?"

"Two dates."

"Really? That's good shit." Dorey handed Tara a glass of wine. "Spill it."

"Oh, no thanks."

"You're not drinking now? Since when?"

"Geoffrey doesn't drink."

"Mutherfuckit. Tara, don't go all chameleon on me. I was just beginning to like you."

"Hey, what's that supposed to mean?" Tara crossed her arms.

"Dammit I'm serious. From what you've told me every time you've been into a guy you change for him. You try to be what you think he wants you to be or you pretend to like what he likes. You change your personality just to keep a man."

"No I don't."

"Think about it. You just did it; a perfect example

actually. You won't have a glass of wine with me because your new man doesn't drink. When have you ever turned down free wine?"

"That's not true. I mean…well, it's not intentional. But I guess a part of me feels that if I'm really myself he might not like me. Or, if I don't like what he likes, then he'll find someone else who has more in common with him."

"I know."

"But doesn't everyone do that? I mean, we all try to be our best selves and look for things we have in common, right? You know, put our best foot forward?"

"Sure. But not at the expense of giving up a part of your identity."

"I'm not sure I follow."

"You're a people pleaser, Tara. You're nice and kind and sweet and I love you to pieces, but you gotta stop being a fucking door mat."

"Ouch! And I'm not a door mat. I wish people would stop seeing my kindness as a weakness. Just because I look for the good in people and forgive easily doesn't mean I'm weak. I have empathy. I genuinely care and relate to people. I sense other people's emotions and I feel what they're feeling."

"Maybe you care too much."

"Why is that a bad thing?"

"Hey, sorry. Don't get defensive. I'm on your side, remember?" Dorey put her hand on Tara's knee and squeezed it. "Honey, I know you're a sensitive soul and I love that about you. But I don't want you to change who you are at the whim of the wind. You need to stay true to yourself, even if it means making others uncomfortable sometimes.

"But, hey, you know I march to the beat of a different drummer. Take my advice or don't. Just know that it's given with love. I don't want to see you get hurt.

"Now, tell me all about those two hot dates you had with Geoffrey. I'm all ears."

5

Surprise

TARA SAW GEOFFREY'S car sitting in her driveway when she got home from work Wednesday. *What's he doing here? We didn't have any plans that I recall.* She parked in the garage then went out to his car and peered into the passenger side window.

He was leaning back with earbuds in and eyes closed. She tapped on the window.

"You startled me, Tara." Geoffrey opened his door and got out of the car.

"I startled *you*? You're the one parked in my driveway unannounced. How long have you been here?"

"Not long. I was just meditating."

"Did we have plans?"

"Nah, I thought I'd surprise you. Hop in. I want to take you out to dinner."

"Wow, that's nice. Thanks! Let me close up the garage

and I'll be right there."

They had a delicious sushi dinner at Tokyo Table, but when the waiter dropped off the check Geoffrey patted his pockets and said, "Oh no, I think I left my wallet at home."

"No worries, you paid for the first two dinners. Let me get this one."

"Thank you, Tara. I'll have to make it up to you somehow."

"Hmm, I'm sure you'll think of something," she teased.

They held hands as they walked to the parking garage and it made Tara feel warm and tingly. A joyous giggle escaped her lips.

"What's so funny?" Geoffrey asked.

Tara blushed, "I'm laughing at myself that holding hands with you is making me feel like a giggly teenager, that's all."

She squeezed his hand for emphasis.

Geoffrey raised his eyebrow, "Why, Tara, you're blushing. If merely holding hands makes you blush—"

"Silly, right?"

"Not at all. I find it rather endearing."

When they got to the car Geoffrey noticed his left rear tire was flat and dropped Tara's hand. He cursed under his breath and opened the trunk to get out the spare.

"Oh no. I wonder how that happened?"

"These things happen," he sighed. "Don't worry, I'll have it changed and we'll be on the road in no time. I'm not going to let a little flat tire ruin my night."

"You're not upset?"

"Of course not. Life is suffering."

"What?"

"It's from Buddhism. Have you heard the phrase, 'Life is a bowl of cherries?'

"Yeah."

"Well, Buddhism teaches, 'life is a bowl of pits and every now and then you get a cherry.' Meaning to expect that things will go wrong and to be thankful when good things happen."

"That sounds pessimistic."

"Not at all. If anything it's more realistic. Will you hand me that lug wrench?"

As Tara handed him the wrench he looked up and lost his balance. He jerked his head forward and collided with the wrench causing blood to spurt out his nose.

"Oh my gosh! I'm so sorry," Tara rushed to his side. "Are you okay?"

"I'll be fine," he laughed. "I think there's a rag in the trunk."

Tara found the rag and held it to Geoffrey's nose to stop the bleeding. His hands were covered in blood and his shirt was soaked. He laughed again.

"Why are you laughing?"

"You should see your face."

"*My* face? You're the one with the bloody nose."

"Yeah, and you look scared to death. Relax. It's just a little blood. No big deal."

Geoffrey insisted he was fine and finished changing the tire. They drove back to Tara's place listening to the radio each lost in their own thoughts.

Once there, Geoffrey stripped off his shirt and asked Tara to soak it in cold water. He turned on the TV, found a movie to watch, "Red Dragon," and lay down on the couch, shirtless and barefoot. Despite the swollen nose he could have been a centerfold poster—he looked that good.

Tara gave him an ice pack and lay down next to him. She traced the lines of his Adonis-like abs and delicately caressed the samurai tattoo on his shoulder. Kissing proved difficult and she didn't want to injure him further so she rolled over to watch the movie. Laying on his side behind her, he lifted up her shirt and lightly tickled her back. His touch thrilled her and made it difficult to concentrate.

After the movie, it was late and Geoffrey's shirt was still soaking in the sink. Tara got up to put the shirt in the washing machine but he pulled her back down and kissed her.

"What about your nose?"

"It doesn't hurt anymore."

"It's late."

"Then we should go to bed."

They fell asleep in each other's arms and remained touching in some form throughout the night. Tara loved the feel of his skin on hers. She enjoyed being with him, laying with him, the smell of him…everything.

And the sex…wow! She forgot how good it felt to have a man in her bed.

The next morning, they woke up at six-thirty and Tara had to get ready for work. When she got out of the shower Geoffrey was still in her bed. She didn't want to rush him but didn't feel comfortable letting him stay either. *Awkward.*

"Do you want anything? Coffee? Breakfast?" she asked, hoping to rouse him.

"I don't drink coffee."

"Good. Me either. What about breakfast?"

"I usually have a protein shake and head to the gym."

"Sorry, I don't have any protein powder," Tara buttoned her blouse and cleared her throat. "I don't want to be rude but I have to get to work."

"No worries, I'll just let myself out." Geoffrey made no attempt to get out of bed.

Flustered, Tara looked at the clock, then back at Geoffrey. "Actually, would you mind leaving now? The door has to be locked with a key and I don't have a spare, so…"

"Tara, are you kicking me out?" Geoffrey teased.

"Yeah, sorry."

"It's all good," he grinned. He grabbed his jeans, got out of bed, and stopped. "Where's my shirt?"

"Oh no. I left it in the washing machine all night. There's no time to dry it and it's wrinkled." *What else could go wrong? I have to leave NOW.*

"Tara, it's okay. Calm down," he rolled his eyes. "You look like you're about to cry, geesh. I have an extra t-shirt in my gym bag. And I always keep my bag in the car. It's okay, really. Just give me my shirt and I'll be on my way."

Tara ran to the washing machine, which was in the garage, pulled out Geoffrey's wet shirt, put it in a plastic bag and handed it to him. Fortunately, he followed her out so she locked the door and headed toward her car.

"Hey, so how about we—"

"Sorry, Geoffrey, I gotta go now or I'm gonna to be late. I'll call you, okay?" Tara got in her car and shut the door, but rolled down the window.

"Sure. Yeah, okay." Geoffrey knelt down and gave Tara a quick kiss through the window, then watched her drive away. Still shirtless, he finally got in his car and drove away, too.

6

Falling

AT WORK, TARA couldn't get Geoffrey off her mind. *Has it only been three dates?* She knew it was too soon but she was already developing feelings for him. *Here I go again, thinking with my heart and not my head.*

"Tara? TARA!" Mandy yelled. Mandy was the new 2nd A.D. She stood at the door to the classroom with her hand on her hip waiting for a response. Tara had two students today, Chad and Zoey, 14 and 12, who played the children of the main character in the new TV show Tara worked on. The parody was created to make fun of the 'wife' shows, *Desperate Housewives* and *The Real Housewives of Orange County*. But when *The Good Wife* aired a few months ago as an instant hit, the producers quickly changed the name of their spoof to *The Bad Wife*. It premiered October 16 on Fox to high ratings.

"Sorry, I was distracted. What's up, Miranda?"

"We need the kids on set."

"Oh, of course. Right away. Come on, guys. It's showtime."

Chad and Zoey put down their homework, grabbed their water bottles and followed Tara to set. They had the routine down by now and everyone got along. Plus, they took direction well. They were bright and talented and great to work with. Sometimes Tara's job seemed too good to be true. She loved it here.

While the kids were on set Tara's responsibilities were reduced mainly to keeping an eye on the time and making sure the young actors were comfortable and safe. Not needed for the moment Tara let her thoughts drift again.

What do I like about Geoffrey? Let's see...he's intelligent and articulate; attractive, I mean, extremely hot; kind and compassionate; affectionate; healthy and into fitness; and he knows a lot about working out and martial arts. He's good for me. I could learn a lot from him and I think he'll make me a better person.

Tara's phone buzzed. It was Geoffrey. *Why is he calling me at work?* She stepped off set and into the studio's hallway to take the call.

"Hello?"

"Who's Kevin?"

"Geoffrey? What are you talking about?"

"Tara, who the hell is Kevin?"

"I don't know what you're—wait. Kevin who?"

"He posted a heart on your Facebook page with some weird comment about hearts and love."

"Oh, that Kevin," she laughed. "Sorry, it was out of context. He's a friend from work. Nobody to worry about."

"Why is he posting hearts on your page, Tara?"

"I don't know. He's harmless. Don't worry about it."

"Of course I'm worried about it, Tara. We barely know

each other. How do I know I can trust you? How do I know you're not seeing other men behind my back?"

"You're right. You don't. I'm sorry you don't feel you can trust me. We've only had three dates. While they've been incredible and I've grown close to you in a very short time, the reality is that we don't know each other very well. Maybe this is going too fast."

"So, you really don't have anything going on with Kevin?"

"No. You need to trust me on this. I gotta go. I'm at work. I'll call you later."

"Tara?"

"What?"

"Why would he post hearts on your page if nothing is going on between you two?"

"I told you, I don't know. I haven't even seen the post yet. I really have to go now. Oh, and Geoffrey?"

"What?"

"Kevin is gay. Maybe you should dig a little deeper before you accuse me of cheating on you."

She ended the call and stormed back into the studio.

Later that night, Geoffrey showed up on Tara's doorstep with a card and an apology.

"Geoffrey, you need to stop just showing up like this. I'm not ready for you to meet my daughter yet."

"Is she here?"

"No, she's at her dad's this week."

"Then what's the problem? Don't you like surprises?"

"I do but...never mind, come in. We need to talk anyway."

"How about a kiss first?" he beckoned.

After a brief kiss Tara led him to the couch where they sat down and talked about sex and expectations. She felt she'd slept with him too soon and that they were moving too fast. She asked him how he felt.

"I'm falling in love with you," Geoffrey said as he reached for Tara's hand. Her eyes grew wide but she didn't say anything. She let Geoffrey continue to talk. "When I'm not with you you're all I think about. If you're worried about sex we don't have to have sex every time we see each other. I just want to be with you."

"That's sweet, but isn't this happening too fast? I have feelings for you, too, but there's still so much we don't know about each other. Don't you think we should slow down?"

"Well, professionally speaking, there is no 'magic formula' for how long a couple should date before getting married. In some arranged marriages the couples don't meet until their wedding day."

"Marriage?" Tara took her hand back. "Why are we talking about marriage?"

"It was just an example, Tara. What I mean is it's neither right nor wrong to fall for someone fast. Everyone is wired differently. Love at first sight does exist and some people know within twenty minutes of meeting their future mate that he or she is the love of their life. There are studies to back this."

"Seriously? Do you think I'm your future mate?"

"Quite possibly. I can definitely see a future with you. Are you open to moving away from Tustin? The schools in my area are excellent and Jalina would love it there."

"Your area? You mean Newport Beach? I haven't even been to your house yet and you haven't met Jalina. This is just talk, right? We're not making plans to move in toge—"

"Of course, silly. We're just talking."

"Good, because I'm not ready for anything like that yet. I've only been divorced a few months and moving Jalina to a new school, away from her friends, is not a good idea right now. I might need us to slow down a bit."

"Tara, you're so serious. I'm talking about the distant future. Don't worry, we have lots of time to get to know each other and we'll take it as slowly as you need to."

"Good. Thank you, Geoffrey. It's important to me that you know I'm not ready for anything serious. I don't think my daughter is ready for me to be dating right now, either."

"I understand. Let's go upstairs and fool around. Nothing too serious, I promise," he teased.

But during sex this time it felt like making love. He was tender and passionate. Their bodies moved together in a synchronized rhythm like they were made for each other, fitting together perfectly. Tara thought about a future with Geoffrey and it frightened and thrilled her at the same time. *I should be alarmed that he's moving so fast; that he's so intense. But it also feels really good to be wanted.*

Tara glanced up at Geoffrey already asleep. *Could I love this man? Could I love him enough to want to spend the rest of my life with him? Hmm...* Smiling, she drifted off with her head on his chest as he held her. She allowed herself to dream of the possibility of a future with Geoffrey. At that moment she felt loved—and safe.

7

Laser Tag

GEOFFREY SPENT THE night at Tara's three nights in a row. When Tara got home from work Friday she found him waiting for her in the driveway telling her how much he'd missed her all day. She loved the attention. Things were going so well she decided it was time to introduce him to her daughter.

It was Saturday and Joe had to drop Jalina off a day early. He had another business trip to jet off to. This time, London.

Tara thought a fun activity would be a great icebreaker and the perfect introduction for Jalina and Geoffrey. She called Laser Quest and reserved a session of laser tag for that afternoon. Then she called Nicolee, Skyler's mom, and invited Skyler. She knew Jalina would have more fun if she could bring her best friend.

After everyone geared up with their black canvas vest

packs and laser guns, the Laser Quest employee went over the rules. The group of twelve players recited a pledge of fairness and safety before launching into the dark maze-like arena.

Lit only with black lights and strobes the maze would have been eerie if not for the brightly painted neon designs on the black walls. Combined with swirling fog and pulsing loud music, the electric atmosphere encouraged a good amount of adrenaline to course through their veins.

Jalina and Skyler paired up against Geoffrey and Tara mostly tagging Geoffrey as often as possible. They had fun ambushing him with shrieks and giggles every time one of them hit their mark. He was a good sport about it and took it in stride.

Among the other eight players in their session was Mike Crenshaw, a kid from school, and his dad. Mike was a known bully and Jalina and Skyler steered clear of him until Mike's dad recognized her.

"Hey, Jalina, you're in the same class with Mikey, right?" Mike's dad greeted her.

"Mikey?" Jalina giggled.

"Shut up, Ja-*meana*," Mike bristled.

"I'm sorry...I didn't get your name," Tara interjected.

"Crenshaw...Bart Crenshaw. But most people just call me Crenshaw. I help out at the kids' school every once in a while and have volunteered in Mikey and Jalina's class a couple times. The kids call me Mr. Crenshaw." He extended his hand and Tara shook it.

"Nice to meet you, Mr. Crenshaw. Well, see you out there." Tara motioned to Jalina and Skyler to follow her and they headed up the ramp.

Fiercely competitive, Crenshaw and son racked up their 'kills' by repeatedly tagging Jalina and Skyler to the point of harassment. When Jalina complained to Geoffrey he took matters into his own hands.

"Hey, buddy," Geoffrey got in Crenshaw's face and poked him with his laser gun. "You think it's funny to pick on little kids?"

"Nah, man. It's just a game. Lighten up."

"You better lighten the fuck up," Geoffrey whispered, then shoved him back. "Why don't you pick on someone your own size and leave these girls alone?"

"Sure, man. Whatever you say," Crenshaw mumbled.

"And apologize."

"Sorry, girls. I didn't mean to ruin your game. No hard feelings?" Crenshaw disappeared down the ramp and left them alone the remainder of the game.

"Thank you, Geoffrey! You're my hero," Jalina beamed at him. She and Skyler ran through the maze to another part of the arena. Tara followed them to make sure they were okay.

Geoffrey went down the ramp in search of Crenshaw.

He spotted Crenshaw alone kneeling in a dark corner and pointing his laser gun out the cut-out window.

Geoffrey glanced around to make sure nobody was watching. Without a soul in sight he seized his opportunity and tackled Crenshaw to the ground. He landed a few kidney punches under Crenshaw's vest then kicked him in the groin for good measure.

"Stay away from Jalina and her mom or next time you won't be so lucky." Geoffrey stood up and left the roughed-up Crenshaw cowering in the corner, weeping into his hands.

When Tara tucked Jalina into bed that night, they talked about what a fun day they'd had. Nala curled up at Jalina's feet as Tara stood up to leave.

"Mommy?"

"Yes, sweetie?"

"I like Geoffrey. He's really nice. He stood up for Skyler and me against mean old Mr. Crenshaw. I approve."

"Oh, you approve, huh?" Tara laughed. "Well, good. I'm glad you like him. I like him, too."

"Good night, Mommy. I love you."

"I love you, too, sweetheart. Good night. Sweet dreams."

Geoffrey waited for Tara downstairs. When she came down they sat and talked in the living room a for few minutes then he announced he better head home.

"Your daughter's here now. I don't want to make anything awkward in the morning for her."

"Thank you, Geoffrey, I really appreciate that."

"She's a good kid. You did a great job raising her and should be proud."

"Thanks. She is a good kid, but I don't know how much I had to do with it."

"Nonsense. Give yourself some credit for being a good parent. You'd be surprised how many bad parents are out there. I hear their sob stories in my office every day." He shook his head then pulled Tara into his embrace. They exchanged an affectionate kiss, then he added, "I'll call you tomorrow. Sweet dreams, babe."

8

Thanksgiving

"HAPPY THANKSGIVING, TARA," Geoffrey smiled as she opened the door. They'd been dating three weeks and it was time to meet his family. Joe asked to have Jalina this year so he could take her to visit his grandparents; Tara's family lived too far away. Geoffrey invited Tara to spend the holiday with his family. It was two o'clock and he was right on time, as usual.

Excited and nervous to meet Geoffrey's family, Tara hoped they would provide some insight into his character. He answered her questions but never fully in-depth and was masterful at changing the subject. He shared aspects of his therapy practice with her but pointed out he wasn't allowed to divulge too much for he didn't want to breach patient confidentiality. He spoke often about his mother, and said they were very close, but Tara sensed he was holding something back.

Plus, she hadn't even been to his house yet. He always drove to her condo and was usually there waiting for her before she even got home from work. Whenever she hinted about going to his house he was evasive and made up excuses. *Was he hiding something?* She needed reassurance and hoped his family would enlighten her.

They drove to his aunt and uncle's house in Laguna Hills. The modest, one-story home was filled with more people than Tara had expected and she was a little taken aback. Geoffrey neglected to tell her how many people would be there. How would she be able to have meaningful conversations with anyone in a crowd this large?

"Tara, it's so wonderful to meet you. We've heard so much about you. Please, come in, come in. Here, let me take your jacket," the smiling woman said as she ushered them in. "Oh, I'm so sorry. Where are my manners? I'm Jeff's, er, Geoffrey's Aunt Penny." She hugged Tara, took her jacket, and scooted off down the hallway.

Before Tara could ask, Geoffrey immediately whispered, "Jeff is a nick name only my family calls me. Aunt Penny is my dad's sister and all the family members here today are from his side. What's left of my mom's family is in Japan."

"Why didn't you tell me there'd be so many people here today?"

"I didn't know. Sometimes the cousins show up, sometimes they don't. Everyone's sort of scattered and we don't always get together on holidays like this. Don't worry, I won't quiz you on everyone's names," he winked and squeezed her hand. "Ready to meet Mom?"

"Sure," she gulped.

Geoffrey worked his way through the crowd over to the small clump of people on the back patio with Tara in tow. She recognized his mother instantly. She was the only Japanese woman there, poised and diminutive among a sea of tall, fair-skinned and blue-eyed Caucasians.

"How lovely to meet you, Tara. I'm Erica, this is my husband Fred, daughter Wendy, her husband Alex, and their sons Liam and Zak." Erica extended her hand and slightly bowed.

"Lovely to meet you, too," Tara smiled as she shook Erica's hand. "I've heard a lot about you."

"And I've heard a great deal about you as well."

Their eyes locked for a moment and Tara was about to say something when Geoffrey's little sister Wendy threw her arms around Tara in a warm embrace, "Welcome, honey! We're so happy that you're here. You must tell me all about yourself."

Wendy put her arm around Tara and said, "I'm stealing her for a bit. You don't mind, do you, Jeffy?"

Geoffrey cleared his throat and smiled, "No, not at all. By all means, you should show her around."

They walked back into the din of the house and Wendy steered Tara toward the dining room. They found a quiet corner and sat down.

"You'll have to excuse my mother. She comes across cold at first and it takes her a bit to warm up to people but she has a big heart."

"Oh, I didn't think she seemed cold."

"Sure you didn't. It's okay, you can be straight with me. I saw the death stare she gave you. But don't worry, her bark is worse than her bite."

"Why did she look at me like that? Does she not approve of Geoffrey's dating me?"

"Oh no, it's nothing like that. She's the least racist person I know. As you can see, she married a white guy whose roots are in Denmark. Geoffrey and I are half Japanese and half Danish. I married a Chinese guy, so my kids are even more mixed. And my mom adores them.

"Anyway, it's not that she doesn't like you. She just doesn't know you yet and she's wary of strangers."

"Was she born in the states?"

"Funny you should ask. Actually, yes. But it's a very sad story. Come on, let's go for a walk. The fresh air will do us good."

Wendy stood up, reached out to Tara, and held her hand as they weaved through the crowd of happy, laughing people and headed out the front door.

Dropping Tara's hand when they got outside Wendy hugged herself, adjusting to the cool breeze in the late afternoon sun. They sauntered down the Palm tree-lined sidewalk and Wendy began her story.

"My grandparents immigrated to America in 1940, just as Japan got involved in the War. The United States wasn't in it yet and, of course, they had no idea what was about to happen or that it would turn into World War Two. They thought they'd be safe here.

"In 1942, they were forced out of their Los Angeles home and sent to a Japanese-American Internment Camp over two hundred miles away in Manzanar. My grandmother was pregnant with my mother. She already had a baby and a two-year-old, both boys.

"The conditions were brutal and food was scarce. By the time my mom was born in October there were more than 10,000 Japanese Americans crowded into the 500 barracks. To break it down—and I've done the research—there were about eight people assigned to each twenty-by-twenty-five-foot room. They shared one oil stove, a single hanging light bulb, and a few cots, blankets, and mattresses.

"There was no plumbing in the barracks and they had no privacy. There were separate toilet areas for men and women but they were communal; just rows of toilets and showers with no partitions or stalls."

"Wait. Your mother was born in an Internment camp?"

"Yes."

"That's terrible. I can't even begin to imagine…how long was her family kept there?"

"They were released three years later in 1945. But that's not all. Like I said, food was scarce. There were a few crowded mess halls where everyone ate their meals. But the babies were starving and my grandmother wasn't producing enough milk to nurse.

"My grandfather, Kaito Higashi, knew she needed more to eat so he snuck food to her. He gave her some of his rations. But it wasn't enough. He felt he was a burden to his family. He was just another mouth to feed and unable to care for them. This brought him great shame and sadness.

"He felt his wife needed all her energy to take care of the babies and herself. He didn't want her to worry about him. He did the only honorable thing he knew to do. But you have to understand, Japanese culture was very different back then."

"What did he do?" Tara was afraid to ask.

"He committed hara-kiri using his grandfather's samurai sword. It is a Japanese ritual suicide that was considered an honorable method of taking one's life. My grandfather sacrificed himself for the greater good and his family's well-being. He truly believed he was doing them a favor and that honor would be restored to them.

"He left behind a young bride and their three small children. That youngest child, her Japanese name Eriko, grew up to be Geoffrey's and my mother. Grandfather was only twenty-six."

"Wendy, I'm so sorry. That is so tragic."

"I know, it's awful. So, my mom grew up with that over her head. My grandmother blamed my mom for my grandfather's death. And what was her crime? She was born."

"I don't know what to say…" a stunned Tara said.

"It's better if you don't say anything. My mom would kill me if she knew I told you. Ha ha, funny choice of words. But seriously, don't tell Geoffrey either. He's very protective of her and might not want you to know." Wendy glanced at her watch. "Oh, crap. We'd better get back. It's nearly time to eat and people will be looking for us."

"Hello ladies, where have you two been? Tara, you look freezing. How long have you been out there?" Geoffrey asked as soon as they walked in the front door.

"Relax, bro, we just went for a walk and had a nice chat. I'm enjoying getting to know Tara. It's been so long since you've brought anyone around and—"

"Thanks, Wendy, I'll take it from here," Geoffrey waved her away. "Sorry about my sister. I hope she didn't talk your ear off. Her name should be Windy, as in long-winded," he laughed.

"She didn't talk my ear off. I think she's great. I really like your sister," Tara replied.

"Okay everyone, the kitchen is open," Aunt Penny declared. "We're doing this buffet-style, so come get your plate and line up. Dinner is served."

They stayed until 9:30 when Geoffrey nudged Tara, kissed her, and asked, "Want to get out of here?"

"Sure," she said, her cheeks flushed from the public kiss.

They grabbed their jackets from the guest room and said their goodbyes. After wading through an onslaught of hugs they were finally out the door heading toward the car.

While they were eating the Thanksgiving feast, Tara counted twenty-six people, including kids. That was a lot of people to meet all at once and she was exhausted.

On the way back to her place, Geoffrey asked, "So, what do you think of my crazy family?"

"I don't think they're crazy. They were warm, friendly, and very welcoming. It was a wonderful day and I enjoyed talking to everyone—especially Wendy. We had a great talk. What's the age difference between you two?"

"Really? What did you two talk about?"

"You know, mostly girl talk. How old is she?"

"We're seven years apart. She's 37."

"Thank you so much for including me and letting me be a part of this special day with your family. I really enjoyed meeting them."

"Good, I'm glad. I'm confident they enjoyed meeting you too."

In bed Geoffrey told Tara he was thankful for her. Then he said, "But actions speak louder than words, so now it's time to show you."

As they made love all Tara could think was *Wow*. He seemed to know exactly what her body needed. Geoffrey was impassioned, constantly kissing and caressing her. She couldn't remember the last time she'd experienced so much passion directed toward her. It made her feel loved and adored. Geoffrey oozed sensuality and she was hooked.

9

Christmas Lights

EARLY THE NEXT morning, Geoffrey woke Tara up with soft tickles up and down her back. She smiled and stirred but didn't want to wake up from a good dream. She rolled over and tried to fall back to sleep.

Undeterred, he kissed her neck, ears, and face, settling on her lips.

"Mmm, what time is it?" Tara asked, not wanting to open her eyes.

"Six. Does it matter?" Geoffrey was in a feisty mood and pulled the pillow out from under her head.

"Hey, I was sleeping."

"I see. Should I let you go back to sleep then?"

"Yes."

"Wrong answer."

He straddled her and tickled her until she laughed so hard, she couldn't catch her breath.

"Okay, I'm up," Tara managed, in between giggles. "Mercy!"

Geoffrey stopped tickling her.

This time when they made love there was a ferocity to it. He was less gentle, more urgent, even rough. Tara wasn't sure she liked it and wondered what brought on the change.

After Geoffrey left Tara picked up Jalina and Nala at Joe's. They'd agreed Tara would pick her up Friday morning while Joe was at work, to allow her to sleep in.

Jalina was excited to decorate the condo for Christmas. It would be Tara's first Christmas on her own, and without Joe, in fifteen years. It was a bittersweet realization.

They hurried home and got all the Christmas boxes out of the garage.

"Mommy, can I test the twinkle lights and plug them all in?"

"Sure, sweetie, that's a good idea. That way, if we need more we can run to the store real quick."

Tara unpacked various snowmen, angels, and snow globes and looked around the living room strategizing where to put everything. She pushed the couch over about a foot to the left to make room for the tree.

"None of these light strands are working!" Jalina hollered from the hallway.

"None of them? That's odd."

"None of them. What are we going to do?"

"Something must have happened to them in the move, I guess. Huh," Tara sighed. "No worries. Come on, get your coat. There's a big sale at Target, especially for Christmas lights."

"Yay! Sorry, Nala, you have to stay here. But we won't be gone long, I promise." Jalina scratched behind Nala's ears then followed her mom to the car.

At Target, her arms loaded with boxes of twinkle lights and garland, Tara mumbled to herself, "Why didn't I get a cart?"

"It's okay Mommy, I'll go get one," Jalina said over her shoulder as she ran off in the direction of the shopping carts.

While waiting for Jalina, Tara saw Mr. Crenshaw looking at the fake Christmas Trees on display.

She staggered toward him with her cumbersome load. "Mr. Crenshaw? Hi, do you remember me? I'm Jalina's mom. We met at Laser tag two weeks ago and—"

Crenshaw blanched and froze as if afraid. As Tara tried to figure out his bizarre reaction, he bolted past her, knocking a couple boxes of lights out of her arms.

"I just saw Mr. Crenshaw running out of the store," Jalina said as she skipped up with the cart.

"Yeah, it was the strangest thing," Tara said, emptying an armload of wares into the cart. "I just said hi to him and he dashed out past me. His face was so white you'd think he'd seen a ghost."

"Huh, I wonder why?"

"Yeah, me too sweetie. Me too."

Tara and Jalina admired their handiwork. They gazed at the Christmas Tree, lovingly decorated with many specialty ornaments and a few handmade ones. For filler, they used red glass ball ornaments, which added a nice touch of vivid color. It created a regal, festive look and they were pleased.

Mother and daughter were chatting away in the kitchen rinsing off the dinner dishes and cleaning up when the doorbell rang.

"I'll get it," Tara said as she dried off her hands.

"Who's here?" Jalina asked.

"Oh, sorry, I forgot to tell you. I asked Geoffrey to stop by tonight so we could show off our beautifully decorated house."

"Oooh, he's gonna love it."

Tara opened the door, then scooted back and stood underneath the archway to the dining area.

"Babe? What are you doing?" Geoffrey asked as he walked in. "Hey, the place looks great. You did a nice job decorating for Christmas. It's very... festive."

"I had help." Tara winked at him and pointed toward the ceiling. Jalina peered around the corner.

"Oh, mistletoe!" he exaggerated. "I guess I better kiss you now." He smiled and planted a big kiss on Tara. They could hear Jalina's giggles of glee from the kitchen.

"Hi, Jalina," Geoffrey called to her.

"Hi, Geoffrey," Jalina bounded out of the kitchen. "Do you like our decorations? The mistletoe was my idea."

"I love them, Jalina. You guys did a great job. Give me a high five."

Jalina rolled her eyes, "Silly, that's for little kids." But she slapped his hand anyway.

Just then they heard a horn honk outside.

"Skyler's here. Gotta go. Love you, Mom. See ya later Geoffrey. Bye, Nala!" Jalina grabbed her waiting backpack, waved, and ran out the door.

Tara followed her out and waved at Nicolee as they drove away.

10

Nala

NALA WHIMPERED AND whined all night.

She usually slept with Jalina, and even stayed with Jalina at her dad's. It was great for Nala because Jalina walked her as soon as she got home from school. The few times Jalina couldn't take her Nala slept on Tara's bed. And, occasionally, Tara took Nala to work with her. The sweet dog disliked being alone and had always slept with one of her people—until now.

Geoffrey had never slept with pets on the bed before and thought it odd and unsanitary. He asked Tara if the dog could sleep on the floor. This was the first night it became an issue since Nala had been with Jalina the other times Geoffrey spent the night. But Jalina didn't take the dog with her to Skyler's this time because they were going straight to a movie and couldn't leave Nala in the car that long.

Tara ended up having to shut Nala out of her bedroom. She tried to get her to sleep on Jalina's bed but, without Jalina, it didn't work. She couldn't get her to sleep on the floor in her room, because she just jumped up on the bed. Nala didn't understand why she was being forced out and it broke Tara's heart. She tossed and turned all night and listened to Nala's pitiful pleas and pacing outside the door.

At four o'clock in the morning Nala started barking. Tara got up, took her outside to pee, then brought her back to Jalina's room and stayed with her. At last, Nala slept and the house was quiet.

Blurry-eyed, stressed out and miserable, Tara got up at seven and made breakfast. She worried Geoffrey would be upset and wanted to appease him. As soon as he came downstairs she launched into a full-scale apology for Nala's behavior.

"It's okay, don't worry about it," he said. He sat down at the table and they ate in silence.

Geoffrey pulled out his phone and read something, then set the phone down on the table. After a pause he said, "Tara, I don't know you."

"What do you mean?"

"Well, I just think we're very different."

"Is this because of Nala? Because you don't like her on the furniture?"

"No. It has nothing to do with the dog. She can be trained to stay on the floor," he sighed.

"What then?"

"I was talking to my mother upstairs a few minutes ago and she asked me some questions about you that I couldn't answer. It made me realize there's a lot about you I don't know."

"Like what? You can ask me anything."

"Like, what do you do with your free time? What are

your hobbies? What do you do to stay active?" He paused and looked at her. "Tara, I'm attracted to fit, active people. You don't work out. I don't even think you like to work out. You talk about wanting to lose weight but then you don't do anything about it."

"You're right. I need to work out."

"Be proactive. Remember?"

"Yes, I remember."

"Do you have a plan?"

"I was looking into a couple different gyms deciding which one to join."

"You haven't even joined a gym yet?"

"Well…no."

"What do you do with your free time when I'm not here?"

"What free time? You're always here. Why don't we ever hang out at your house? Why haven't you ever invited me over there?"

"We're not having this discussion again." He pushed his chair out and stomped upstairs.

Tara got up and cleared off the table. She threw the dishes in the sink with too much force and broke a glass, cutting her finger. "Ouch!"

Geoffrey came back downstairs fully dressed. "What happened? Are you okay?"

"No, I'm not okay. You were rude to me just now. I felt attacked."

"I know. I'm so sorry, Tara." He reached out to touch her but she pulled away, still holding a paper towel to her finger. "I'm just tired and cranky, that's all. I'm under stress at work that has nothing to do with you. I had no right to talk to you like that. Do you forgive me?"

He pulled her into an embrace, then kissed her longingly.

"Let's get that finger taken care of." He led her upstairs

to the bathroom and got out the band-aids then rinsed her finger under the running water. All the while telling her how beautiful she was and stroking her hair.

She couldn't hide her feelings from him. She wanted to stay mad at him but felt herself softening more with each stroke of his hand on her hair. She felt transparent, like he could see everything she thought and felt. Just looking at him broke her down like he was some kind of instant truth serum.

"I forgive you," she whispered.

11

Three Little Words

DURING DINNER THAT night Geoffrey seemed distant and distracted. Jalina was there so Tara was hesitant to ask him about it. But when he checked his phone for the third time, clearly distraught, she finally asked, "Is everything all right?"

"Yeah, it's all good. Just some trouble at the house. Nothing for you to worry about."

"What trouble? What's going on?"

"Well, I wasn't going to say anything yet. That is, until I knew for sure, but I've been meeting with a Realtor to sell the house. She had an inspection done and now it has to be tented for termites. So…I need to stay in a hotel a few days. The one I had booked just emailed me back that they're full."

Before Tara had a chance to think, Jalina blurted out, "You don't have to stay in a hotel, you can stay with us!"

"Really?" he looked at Tara. "Isn't it a little soon?"

"Well, it's just for a few nights. Right?" Tara looked at Jalina. "Are you sure you want Geoffrey to stay with us, honey?"

"Yeah, it'll be fun," she grinned. "We can watch movies and eat popcorn."

"Oh, like you do on your sleepovers with Skyler? Um…" Geoffrey was at a loss for words.

"Yeah. You like movies, right Geoffrey?"

"Absolutely. I love movies."

"Then it's settled. I'm gonna go call Skyler and tell her. May I be excused now?"

"Of course, sweetie. Just take your plate to the kitchen first, please."

"Okay," Jalina cleared her dishes and skipped upstairs with Nala trailing her. They watched her go upstairs.

Geoffrey tried to fill the awkward silence between them, "Babe, dinner was delicious. The salmon was so succulent, and the green beans—"

"Nice try. I mean, thank you, but why didn't you tell me you're selling your house? That's a pretty big thing to keep from me, don't you think?"

"Like I said, I wanted to wait to tell you until I knew for sure."

"Knew for sure what?"

"Until I knew for sure how I felt about you," he paused and took a deep breath, then gazed into Tara's eyes. "I thought it would be better for Jalina if I bought a house up here closer to her school so she wouldn't have to change schools or move away from her friends. And then I could make it official and ask you to move in with me…or ask you to marry me."

"What?" Tara was at a loss for words.

"Tara, this month with you has been amazing. You're all

I think about. I'd move in here right now just so I could be with you all the time, but I want to be respectful of your daughter. That's why I haven't spent the night when she's been here. But now that she wants me to, that changes things. Maybe—"

"Maybe what? You can move in right now? No, I'm not ready for that. Jalina's not ready for that. I don't—"

"No, of course I'm not moving in yet. Don't worry, it's your call. I'll take this as slow as you need me to. But make no mistake—I don't take our relationship lightly. My intentions are to marry you. I am committed to you. I love you."

Tara sat back at his revelation. Then slowly, "I love you, too, Geoffrey. I've been falling in love with you since we met. But moving in? It's just too fast. I don't…I need to think about this." Tara got up and busied herself by clearing the table and doing the dishes.

Geoffrey walked into the kitchen and stood for a moment watching Tara at the sink. He went over to her and put his arms around her from behind. He nuzzled her ear, "I'm not breaking up with you ever."

He kissed her neck and slid his hands up to her breasts.

"You're stuck with me," he whispered.

She closed her eyes and leaned into him. Her body responded to his touch as she turned around to kiss him.

"Hey, watch it!"

She opened her eyes to see a startled Geoffrey, wet and soapy. In her bliss, she'd forgotten to let go of the soapy dish rag first.

A second later, they'd both gone from aroused to amused and were soon laughing uncontrollably in the middle of the kitchen.

In bed that night after Geoffrey fell asleep, Tara studied

him. The moonlight through the window was enough for her to behold the details and wonders of his sleeping face. Such a beautiful man. She knew 'beautiful' wasn't usually applied to men, but that was the only word she could think of that fit.

She figured she'd never tire of looking at him, touching him, breathing him in…listening to his voice…loving him and making love with him. She was in awe that he chose her, that he loved her. She didn't know what she'd done to deserve such a wonderful man, but she felt very lucky.

12

Joe

TARA WAS IN the kitchen making breakfast when Jalina came downstairs.

"Good morning, Mommy. Is Geoffrey coming to church with us? Yum! Chocolate chip pancakes! Can I help?"

"They're almost ready. You can set the table and get yourself something to drink," Tara slid the spatula under a pancake and flipped it over. "No sweetie, Geoffrey won't be coming to church with us. He doesn't have the same beliefs we do. He'll probably just stay here and sleep in."

"Oh. What does he believe in?"

"Well, he said he's not really religious. He went to Catholic school when he was your age. He was even an altar boy but he didn't understand their doctrine and didn't feel religion was right for him. Now he says he ascribes to the teachings of Buddhism." She put two pancakes on Jalina's plate and walked back into the kitchen, which flowed into the small dining room. Sitting at the table Jalina watched her mother pour more pancake batter on the griddle.

"Mmm, these are delicious!" With a mouthful of pancake, she added, "What's Buddhism?"

"I don't know enough about it to give you a good answer right now. Maybe you can ask Geoffrey sometime?"

"Okay."

"Mmm, what's that *heavenly* smell?" Geoffrey teased as he came downstairs letting Tara know he'd heard their conversation.

"Good morning, Geoffrey. Mommy's making pancakes. Do you want some?"

"I usually have a protein shake in the morning. But okay, maybe just this once."

"You want banana or chocolate chip?" Tara called from the kitchen.

"Just one banana pancake for me, thanks," Geoffrey called back, and sat down at the table with Jalina.

"Mommy says you're not religious. Does that mean you don't believe in God?"

"That's right. I don't believe there's a God."

"What about Jesus? Do you believe in him?"

"Here's your pancake," Tara interjected.

"Thank you," he paused. "I believe Jesus was a man. I think he was a good person and a great teacher, but ultimately just a man. Sort of like Gandhi."

"Who's Gandhi?"

"Okay, Jalina. That's enough questions for now. Go brush your teeth and let's get going," Tara said. Then to Geoffrey, after Jalina ran upstairs, "Sorry about that. She can ask a lot of questions."

"I don't mind. I'll tell her anything she wants to know. As long as it's okay with Mom, of course."

"Thanks. And please don't call me Mom," they both laughed.

A few minutes later, as Tara and Jalina were getting ready to leave, Tara asked, "We're gonna stop by the store and get a few groceries on our way home. Is there anything you'd like me to pick up?"

"Yes, please, how about some holy water?"

"Ha ha, very funny. Have fun with Nala."

"Have fun at church." He gave her a quick kiss and they left.

It was Sunday night and time for Jalina to switch to her dad's house. Joe showed up at six thirty to get her and sent her a text, "I'm here."

He opened the garage door with his clicker then knocked on the door. Jalina let him in through the garage and gave him a big hug.

"What's up, Squirt?" Joe released her and ruffled her hair. "You ready to go?"

"Yep. All set," Jalina replied.

Geoffrey had been upstairs and didn't know Joe was coming over. He heard a man's voice and came down to investigate. He thought Joe had let himself in. For him there was no warning and he found himself face-to-face with Tara's ex for the first time.

"Hey, Geoffrey. It's nice to meet you. I'm Jalina's dad, Joe." Joe extended his hand and Geoffrey shook it.

"Hi, Joe. It's good to meet you too," Geoffrey smiled. "Bye, Jalina. Have a good week at your dad's."

"Thanks, Geoffrey. I'll see ya next weekend. Bye, Mommy. I love you."

"I love you, too, sweetie. Have a great week. I miss you already," Tara said as she hugged her daughter.

"Mommy, you don't have to miss me. Geoffrey's here

now so you won't be lonely anymore."

"What makes you think I'm lonely? I could never be lonely with you around."

"That's what I mean. For when I'm not here. Now you have Geoffrey. Bye!"

"Bye, baby." Tara's heart was full, and her eyes brimmed with tears.

Joe nodded and grabbed Jalina's bag while Jalina grabbed Nala's leash. She turned and waved then the three of them left through the garage and headed toward Joe's car.

Before Tara could get the door closed and turn around Geoffrey stomped down the hall toward the living room.

"What the hell was that?" he nearly exploded.

"Whoa, what are you so upset about?"

"Why does he have a garage door opener to your place? Does he think he can just walk in here whenever he wants? That makes me feel very uncomfortable, Tara. You need to establish boundaries with your ex."

"Hold on. First of all, he didn't just walk in. He texted Jalina, and knocked, and she let him in. Second, he is the father of my child and I trust him. We have joint custody and we both have a key to each other's houses. It makes things much easier because sometimes Jalina forgets her key and...why am I explaining this to you?"

"It's not right. It's not healthy for exes to be friends. You shouldn't have keys to each other's homes. Jalina's old enough to take on the responsibility of carrying her own keys. Let her get locked out a few times. Then she won't forget anymore.

"I don't want him to have that garage door opener either. You need to get it back from him. What if I'm here alone some day and he comes over and does something crazy?"

"What are you talking about? Joe would never do

anything crazy. He's about as violent as a puppy."

"You never know. Passion makes people do crazy things. What if he's jealous of us? What if he wants you back?"

"You've got to be kidding," Tara laughed. "There is no way that will ever happen. Is that what you're worried about? That Joe might still have feelings for me? Trust me, those died a long time ago."

"You'd be shocked at the stories I could tell you, and have told you. Do I need to remind you about what happened to Sheila? You know I've had bad experiences with exes in the past. People are capable of doing horrific things. Just get the garage door opener and key from him, okay?"

"Okay, I'll get them back. I was going to get a key made for you anyway but now you can use Joe's while you're here. But to be clear, you have nothing to worry about. Joe is a good guy and would never do anything crazy or to jeopardize his relationship with our daughter. And as far as his relationship with me goes we have complete closure. There are no ambiguous feelings between us. We're co-parents of Jalina and care about each other's well-being because of our shared history. That's it."

"Still, I'm not comfortable with him coming over here. I don't care if he's a 'good guy.' I have no interest in getting to know him, don't want to be his friend, and don't think you should talk to him either."

Tara bit her lip and tried to see the situation from Geoffrey's point of view. If his ex showed up here would she be jealous, insecure, and uncomfortable? She didn't think so and she didn't understand why Geoffrey was making such a big deal out of it. Joe was nothing like Sheila's ex. Deep in thought, she barely heard him when he started talking again.

"Tara, did you hear me? I said I don't want him coming

over here anymore."

"Look, I'm trying to understand your feelings about this and I don't want you to be uncomfortable here, but I share custody of my *child* with Joe. Are you asking me to pick her up and drop her off all the time? Am I supposed to forbid Joe from ever driving over here to pick up his own daughter?"

"Can't you guys meet at a half way point? Some neutral ground, like a park or store parking lot?"

"Why is that necessary? We take turns driving Jalina to and from her homes. She lives with both of us. We're trying to keep her life as normal as possible. It's called parenting."

"Fine. But next time he has to drive over here to pick her up just have him wait in the car."

"Fine."

13

House Key

THE NEXT MORNING Tara got up and left for work before Geoffrey woke up. She was still upset about the night before and wasn't sure how she felt anymore. How could he be cold one minute, but then affectionate and wonderful the next?

Conflicted, she called Joe at work and asked for her spare key and garage door opener back. She wanted to keep her word and honor Geoffrey's wishes, even if she thought his fears were ridiculous.

Joe's reaction was expected. He laughed and said, "Paranoid much?"

"He's been through a lot. His ex-wife's first husband, and father of her three kids, threatened to kill Geoffrey multiple times. He'd show up at the house, unannounced and high, and demand to see his kids. When he and Sheila were married he'd abused her which is why she left him.

"She had to get a restraining order against him because she feared for her children's safety and there were multiple battles in court over custody and other issues. I guess it got so bad they even had him arrested a few times. He lost his parental rights and Sheila asked Geoffrey to adopt her children, to be their full-time father.

"But her oldest child inherited his father's sociopathic tendencies and got kicked out of multiple schools. He also called the cops a couple times claiming child abuse because he wanted to get rid of Geoffrey and have his mom all to himself. It was too much for Geoffrey to bear and he had to divorce Sheila."

"Wow, sounds like you got yourself a real winner there, Tara."

"It's not Geoffrey's fault that Sheila's first husband was a monster. How was he supposed to know?"

"Gee, I don't know. How long did he date her before he married her? Didn't he meet the guy?"

"I don't know. I've asked Geoffrey before but he doesn't like to talk about it."

"Yeah, I bet he doesn't."

"May I have the key back or not?"

"Of course. You can pick it up tonight if you want. Or, is that allowed?"

"Knock it off. It's not like that."

"Okay, Tara. Whatever you say. Later."

"Oh, one more thing."

"Yes?"

"Next time you come over, would you mind waiting in your car? Geoffrey feels threatened."

Joe laughed, "It just gets better, doesn't it? The therapist who's threatened by all 'ex-husbands' now because he's traumatized. Sounds like he's the one who needs the head shrinker if ya ask me."

"That's not funny."

"Yes it is, Tara. You need to lighten up a little. Are you sure this guy's not a whack job, too?"

"Joe! You don't know him like I do. Just give him time. Once he gets to know you he'll come around. You'll see."

"Right. Can't wait. Just be careful, Tara. And…don't rush into anything."

Tara ended the call and put down her phone. She had an uneasy feeling in her stomach.

When Tara got home from work, there was a vase filled with brightly colored flowers on the table, and an aroma of something cooking in the kitchen. She called out, "Geoffrey?"

"Well, hello, beautiful. How was your day?" he appeared from behind and kissed her. "Do you like the flowers?"

"Yes, they're lovely. Thank you. Where were you just now?"

"I was in the bathroom. What's the matter with you? You seem jumpy."

"Just a strange day at work, that's all. I'm fine. How was your day?"

"Before I answer that, how about we set the table first? Dinner's nearly ready."

Tara headed for the kitchen, "You made dinner?"

"Yes, silly, I can cook. Does that surprise you?"

"Maybe, a little…what did you make?"

"Spaghetti with my special sauce and whole wheat pasta."

"Sounds great. Can't wait to taste it. Thank you, sweetheart."

"My pleasure. Sit down, I'll serve you."

Geoffrey got everything ready, brought out the food, then lit two candles and sat down.

"Flowers, dinner, candlelight? Okay, I give. What's the occasion?"

"I need an occasion to cook a nice dinner for you?"

"Well—"

"Wait, before you answer that, I do want to say something." He took a drink of water. "I owe you an apology. I overreacted last night when I met your ex and I'm sorry. If you say he won't do anything rash, then I believe you."

"Good, I'm glad you came to your senses. And I gave a lot of thought to what you said last night. You have the right to your privacy while you're here and I want you to be comfortable. I called Joe today and the key and garage door clicker will be returned promptly. He said I can come get them tonight if I want."

"Thank you, but that won't be necessary. I don't want you making an extra trip over there just to get the key. It can wait until the weekend when Jalina comes back."

"Okay, as long as you're all right with it. I'll just stop by the hardware store on my way home from work tomorrow and get a key made for you to use while you're here."

"That'd be great. Thank you, Tara. I might be delusional, but even I know Joe's not going to come over here when it's his week with Jalina."

They both laughed and Tara relaxed. What had she been so worried about earlier? Geoffrey apologized for overreacting and everything was put right again. *Joe doesn't know what he's talking about.*

"Thank you for making me dinner tonight; it was delicious and very sweet of you."

"Good, I'm glad you liked it. Shall we do the dishes together?"

"Absolutely. I'll wash, you dry."

Tara's phone rang and she rushed to her bag to answer

it.

"Why are you in such a hurry—"

"Custom ring tone. It's work." She took the call and was on the phone for less than two minutes. She rejoined Geoffrey in the kitchen and picked up a glass to wash.

He looked at her and noticed her grin, "Tara, you look like the Cheshire cat," Geoffrey said, drying off a plate. "What gives?"

"That was work."

"So you said."

"Well, if you'd let me finish…that was work and they changed the shooting schedule around because of some rewrites, so the kids aren't filming the rest of this week."

"And?"

"And, if the kids don't have to be there, neither do I. I have the rest of the week off." Tara couldn't contain her excitement. Although she enjoyed her job getting an unexpected four days off in the beginning of December was a nice treat.

"That's great. Hey, I've got a couple hours free in my schedule tomorrow. I can start training you. That is, if you still want me to."

"Yes, of course I still want you to. I've been doing some exercises on my own and I found the perfect gym, too. They're having a two for one sign up special so we can sign up together. And it's really close."

"But I have a membership at 24 Hour Fitness and I have access to all of them."

"I know, but 24 Hour is too expensive and too crowded for me. This one's better and it's free to add you. I already called and asked them about you training me and they said we only need to sign a waiver."

"Perfect. It's a date."

"So…how should I pay you for training me?" Tara

raised an eyebrow.

"Why, Tara, I do believe you're blushing," Geoffrey chuckled.

"I'm not blushing, I'm flirting," she stuck out her bottom lip and put the plates away.

"Now you're pouting. And if you don't stick that bottom lip back in I'm going to bite it off."

"Hey, I like my bottom lip."

"So do I," he raised his eyebrows at her and winked.

14

Shrinking

TARA LOOKED IN the refrigerator for something to eat. Geoffrey came up next to her and pushed the door closed. "Oh no you don't. No regular breakfasts on training days. Protein shakes only."

"A protein shake?"

"Yep. Are you going to question everything I ask you to do? Or, how about you trust that I might actually know what I'm talking about?"

"Yes, sir."

"Sorry," Geoffrey sighed. "I get worked up about it because fitness is a huge part of my life." He reached for the five-pound container of protein powder above the refrigerator and carried it to the blender. He kept his back to her and scooped some powder into the blender while he talked.

"I've worked out since I was thirteen. It's my biggest

hobby, and it's important to me you take it seriously, too. I want my partner to be in shape." He added almond milk, frozen berries, a tablespoon of peanut butter, and ice cubes to the blender, then pushed the pulse button. "It bothers me that you don't work out consistently. My hope is that this isn't just your first day of training but the first day of a new lifestyle for you."

Geoffrey poured the shake into two shaker cups and handed one to Tara. He lifted his eyes to meet hers and she saw the intensity in them. She took a step back.

"I know," she whispered. "I want that, too. I really do. You inspire me to be a better person. You are such a great role model of a healthy and fit person, the kind of person I aspire to be. I just need you to guide me and coach me on what to do."

"You really want to get in shape?"

"Yes, more than anything. I want to look good for you."

"Okay, but it's going to mean a lot of hard work and sore muscles. And you need to be committed. It will be tough at first but will get easier as you go. The main thing is to work out every day, especially in the beginning. You want to stretch out the muscles you just worked because it helps with recovery and reduces soreness. It also minimizes lactic acid buildup." Geoffrey paused and drank some of his shake. "I'm glad you want to do this, Tara. It means a lot to me."

"I've been wanting to workout for a while now. I know it's good for me and will make me healthier, but I have a lot going on. I'm a single mom with a full-time job and I feel tired all the time. I feel like I don't have time for me, ya know?"

"Those are excuses, Tara. You need to learn how to prioritize and manage your time better. If you have time to sit and watch TV for an hour at night you have time to work out."

"But what about my work schedule and when Jalina is here?"

"If you want it bad enough, you'll find a way, babe. My schedule is pretty flexible right no so I can help out with Jalina if you want. You know, to make sure you get your workouts in."

"Really? Thanks, Geoffrey, that would be a tremendous help," Tara finished off her shake. "You're right. I'm gonna run upstairs and change into my workout clothes right now. I can't wait to get started," she smiled and hugged him. "See, I told you you're good for me."

"Good girl. That's the spirit," Geoffrey grabbed Tara's arm and held it up in a 'winner' pose.

In the car on the way to the gym, Geoffrey went over the rules. "Okay, here's a few things you need to know about proper gym etiquette if you're going to train with me.

"Number one: when I'm training you, I am your trainer, not your boyfriend. You will do as I say, no questions asked.

"Number two: there will be no chit chat or side conversations. We are going there to work, period.

"Number three: don't touch me, hug me, or show affection toward me at the gym. When I'm working out, don't talk to me. If you need to walk past me to get to the weights you want, ignore me. I will help you but I train alone. Again, I am your trainer, not your boyfriend. Treat me with the same respect you would a personal trainer you hired. Got it?"

"Um, sure."

"You're wondering why I sound so harsh?"

"Something like that."

"When I lift weights I listen to loud music and focus on

lifting. I get into a zone and concentrate on being mindful on only weightlifting and form—I lift heavy. Distractions can get me injured. Does that explain it better?"

"Yes, thank you. I got it, Coach. I'm ready."

At the gym, Tara signed the paperwork, paid the fees, got the introductory tour and was ready for her first training session. Geoffrey had her do a twelve-minute warm-up of interval sprints on a stationary bike, then tested her strength with various free weights, kettlebells, dumbbells, and weight training machines.

While on the seated leg press, she stopped mid-push, the fifth rep of the second set, "I can't do anymore. It hurts too much. I'm tired."

"Listen to you whining," Geoffrey scolded. "You're pathetic. You're so lazy and weak. I'm taking time out of my day to do this for you and you're whining and complaining? Of course it hurts. It's supposed to hurt. Ever heard the saying, 'no pain, no gain?' Tara, if you're not going to take this seriously—"

"I am. I'll try harder. Give me another chance. Please?"

"Whatever. Okay, let's see how many push-ups you can do."

"Push-ups? I can't even do one push-up."

"Not with that attitude. Tell yourself you can't and you can't."

"In case you hadn't noticed, I have zero upper body strength. Look at my skinny little arms and teeny tiny wrists. You're right, I am pathetic," Tara sniveled.

"Tara, let me explain something to you. It's as much attitude as it is strength. With the right mental attitude you can achieve any goal you want. Weak or not, if you believed you could take me down right now, you could."

"But how? You're much stronger than me. And you're a blackbelt in Karate and Aikido. I wouldn't stand a chance against you."

"Stand up. I can show you a self-defense move in two seconds that you don't need training or strength to do. As long as you have the right attitude and can focus. You need be make sure you are aware, that you are mindful of the situation. Then this will work on anyone."

"I could take you down with one move?"

"Temporarily, yes."

"Show me, please."

"All you have to do is punch me, or the attacker, in the throat. He'll momentarily choke and not be able to breathe. That's when you either continue to immobilize him further, or run like hell."

"How would I immobilize him further?"

"It's simple. Just remember to hit his soft parts with your hard parts. For example, punch him in the throat with your fist or the heel of your hand, like this." He made a fist and showed her. She copied him and he reminded her to keep her thumb on the outside. He continued, "While the guy grabs his throat, strike him in the solar plexus, the squishy part right here under the ribs, with your elbow."

"Like this?" she touched his throat with her right fist, then elbowed him with her left arm, just above his stomach, between the ribs.

"Good. Yep, just like that. This sets you up nicely for the final blow. Instinctively, he'll bend over slightly, causing his legs to spread. And that's when you kick him in the balls. It's best if you use your knee or shin, because you can drive your weight through the kick without needing strength. But the front of your foot works, too. Just drive it through with enough force."

"Can we practice the kick, too?"

"Not without pads, sweetheart." Geoffrey's eyes bulged and he covered his groin in mock fear. "Sorry, but I value my nuts and have complete confidence that you could gravely injure them without any practice at all." They both laughed.

On the way home, Geoffrey said, "Tara, I'm glad you've decided to take better care of yourself. You're a beautiful woman but you don't take pride in your appearance. You could be stunning.

"I don't want to sound shallow, but the women I've dated take care of themselves. They're fit, fashionable, and put together. They've also all been under forty.

"You're the only woman I've ever dated who's over forty. You're lucky you look so young for your age but you could look so much better. You don't wear makeup, you wear baggy and unfashionable clothing, and your gray roots are showing. It really bothers me because it tells me you don't want to look good for your man."

Tara felt attacked and defensive. She sat in silence and folded her arms across her stomach trying to shrink herself, make herself smaller, as she shrank inwardly. She wanted to get out of the car and away from Geoffrey. *I need to go crawl under a rock somewhere*, her thoughts a jumble of confusion and humiliation.

She didn't understand how he could be so cold and detached, like he didn't care at all. He listed her shortcomings as though he were updating her on the weather. Who was this man? He was hot and cold, Jekyll and Hyde. Tara wanted to scream.

When they got home, Geoffrey showered, dressed, and said he had to go to the office. He mentioned a new client he needed to prepare for.

Tara barely acknowledged him. She went upstairs, got in the shower, and let her thoughts swirl around in her conflicted mind like a tornado. What was she doing with such a narcissistic, belittling man? How could he be so affectionate and loving one day, and so cold and critical the next? Did she really know him? Maybe Joe was right after all. Maybe they were moving too fast.

A few hours later, Geoffrey came back carrying a small paper bag. He was contrite, with an apology at the ready. Tara's eyes flitted to the flowers still on the table and wondered if this was a pattern. She decided to ask him about it.

"Geoffrey, I think we need to talk." She walked over to the couch, sat down and patted the brown leather next to her. "Will you please join me?"

"Before you begin, I want you to have this." He handed her the bag and said, "Open it."

"Whatever's in here doesn't excuse how you treated me earlier. You can't just—"

"I know. And I'll tell you everything, I promise. Just please, open the present."

Tara opened the bag to reveal a black box. She took out the box and opened it. Inside was a Kenneth Cole watch with a black leather strap and a platinum rectangle face. It was stunning. She loved it and felt her resolve weakening, but she wasn't ready to let him off the hook just yet.

"I already have a watch."

"Yes, but not one like this. Besides, didn't you say Joe bought you that watch? Call me old fashioned, but I'd much rather see you in jewelry from me than in jewelry from your ex." He reached for her wrist and took off the watch she was wearing, then put the new one on in its place. "There, it fits perfectly, Tara. What do you think of it?"

"It's beautiful, thank you. But you shouldn't have. There's nothing wrong with my other watch."

"Except for the fact that it's from Joe. It's a reminder to

me. I know you have a past, and he's Jalina's dad. I'm not trying to pretend he doesn't exist. I just don't want to be constantly reminded of it either. Is that wrong? I love you and you're my girl now."

"Okay," she said slowly. "But, if you love me, you have a funny way of showing it."

"I know," he sighed. "It was wrong of me to talk to you like that earlier. At the gym, too. I should never have called you lazy and pathetic. I know you're trying, and I just made it worse by yelling at you."

"Yes, you did. You hurt my feelings."

"I know, and I'm sorry. What I'm about to tell you is not an excuse. I'm just trying to provide an explanation, some insight to why I have these temporary bursts of anger or insanity.

"My mother was a very strict authoritarian with high expectations. Her parenting and teachable moments involved insults and she motivated through fear and intimidation. Her punishments were harsh, to say the least. If I was out of line, or did something she disapproved of, I got the belt, or the hairbrush, or the frying pan, or whatever happened to be near her at the moment."

Tara's eyes watered and she put her hands on Geoffrey's, encouraging him to continue.

"When I'm stressed or frustrated, I tend to mimic her. I become overly critical. And I know what buttons to push and how to hurt people with my words. I'm good at it."

"That's awful. I'm so sorry that happened to you. But I don't understand, you told me that you and your mom are close."

"She's the only mom I have. Plus, she's mellowed with age. By the time I got too big to hit, she got nicer. And my little sister is seven years younger. Wendy was totally spoiled. You'd think we were raised by two different mothers."

"What about your dad? Did he know about the abuse?"

"My dad is the sweetest man you'll ever meet. But he's not too bright. And my mom keeps him down by reminding him of her superior intellect. She's always right and, if he knows what's good for him, he stays out of her way."

Tara held him and he melted into her arms. This beautiful, broken man showed his vulnerability. She wasn't confused anymore and she loved him more for trusting her with his secret.

15

The Flood

TARA WOKE UP early, so sore from the day before she could barely get out of bed. She groaned as she dragged herself downstairs and made her morning protein shake, a ritual she knew would soon become ingrained in her.

She went to the gym alone for day two of her new routine. Geoffrey had given her a thorough workout plan and diet, and she'd written it all down. There were different parts of the body for different days, which is why she could work out every day while giving her muscles time to recover. The two constants every day were abs and cardio. Apparently, abdominal muscles heal and recover faster than other muscles.

Showering quickly at the gym after a good workout, Tara headed to the hair salon. She got four inches cut off and dyed her hair a warm chocolate brown to cover those stubborn grays. She stopped at the drugstore and bought mascara, which she hadn't even owned, then did her makeup in the car. She was excited to show Geoffrey the new and improved Tara. Plus, the scale showed she'd lost three pounds. She figured it was probably water weight, but her jeans were already a little looser.

When Tara came in through the garage she was surprised to see Geoffrey sitting on the couch, watching TV. She figured he'd be at his office and wondered what he was doing home. She was glad she'd had the foresight to put her makeup on in the car.

"Hi, is everything all right?" she asked.

"Wow, Tara, you look beautiful. I love your new hair style. The shorter cut suits you. Come here and let me get a closer look."

She stood before him and he pulled her down onto his lap. He ran his fingers through her hair, kissing her neck, then her lips.

He pulled away, "Hey, you're wearing makeup. I thought your face looked different. You look way younger, but I thought it was because the gray is gone. Baby, you could pass for mid-twenties right now."

"Wow, thanks," Tara giggled. "But, I'm surprised to see you home so early."

"I only had one client today and she cancelled, so there was no reason to go in."

"Oh?"

"Yep. Also, I have a big favor to ask you."

"What is it?"

"Something went wrong when they tented my house. Apparently, a pipe burst and the whole downstairs is flooded."

"Oh no, that's terrible. What about your furniture?"

"They were able to save most of it. And everything upstairs is fine. But the carpet, my couch, ottoman, and matching chair are all ruined. My homeowner's insurance will reimburse me, but it still sucks."

"So...you need a place to stay while they do the repairs?"

"And I was hoping I could move some of my furniture in here, too. Temporarily, of course."

"Sure. Like, what do you need to move over here?"

"I hope I can use your spare room as a home office. I need access to my work files and my office is on the main floor at the house. It all has to be moved out. I also have to clear out the garage and hope you can make room for my boxes and things in your garage?"

"Absolutely, you can stay here as long as you need to. Mi casa es su casa."

"Thank you, honey. You're a lifesaver."

"When do you need me to clear out the spare room?"

"Uh...since there's water all over the first floor, they already moved my office furniture outside. And...since my stuff can't stay outside, I already called the moving truck, so..."

"When, Geoffrey?" Tara demanded.

"They'll be here by noon tomorrow with my stuff."

"Wow, that's not much notice." Tara was shocked, but recovered quickly, "I guess I know what I'll be doing for the rest of the day today."

"Sorry to spring this on you. And I'd love to stay and help, but I gotta get over there to pack things up, deal with the contractors and the realtor, and get ready for the movers in the morning. I'll just stay there tonight and come back with the truck tomorrow, okay?"

"Okay. Looks like we both have our work cut out for us," Tara smiled, trying to be upbeat.

"Thanks, baby. You're the best," he kissed her and gave her a squeeze. "And, Tara, I want you to know I'm taking this very seriously. I'm interested in a future with you.

"I know it's only temporary, but we'll be living together. Sort of like a 'trial move-in,' and if it works, I'll want to marry you. I just thought you should know that. Also, I'm no free-loader. I'll pay you rent. Just tell me what you think is a fair price and I'll give you rent money tomorrow."

"Okay, let me think about it," Tara said, processing this new information.

"Of course. Oh, do you think you could put your dining table and chairs on Craigslist today? Maybe ask fifty bucks for it? My dining table would look so much better in here. It's mahogany and will look great with your décor. You're going to love it. No offense, but this old oak table is a real eyesore. It looks like something out of the seventies."

"No offense taken; it is out of the seventies," Tara laughed. "I got it free when I moved in here. I'll write up an ad now and hopefully it'll be sold by the time your table gets here tomorrow."

"That would be perfect. Okay, I gotta go. See you tomorrow, roomy." Geoffrey kissed Tara goodbye and was out the door.

She watched him leave and stood there for a minute. She needed to wrap her mind around all that just happened. She had a thousand things to do and didn't have a clue where to start.

Four hours later, Tara had emptied out the second closet in her bedroom, cleared four drawers in the dresser, removed all the boxes and clutter out of the spare room and filled five giant trash bags with clothes and stuff for Goodwill.

When she changed the trash liner in the kitchen trash can, she saw her old watch lying in the trash, the one Joe had given her for Christmas years earlier. It made her sad that Geoffrey felt so threatened by him. She tried to understand, but couldn't relate.

Tara didn't have the heart to leave the watch in the rubbish. She picked it out, cleaned it off, and tucked it deep into a bag designated for Goodwill. She couldn't risk Geoffrey finding it, yet knew she could never wear it again.

The reality of her situation was exciting and terrifying. Geoffrey would move in with her the next day. Yes, he had some anger issues but he always apologized. And she would always be quick to forgive.

What was she thinking? Geoffrey was *moving in* with her in less than twenty-four hours and she hadn't told anyone yet. What would Jalina and Joe think? What would Dorey think?

This was all happening so fast. She needed to make some calls.

Her first call was to Jalina, "Hi, sweetie, how was your day?"

"It was great. Rehearsals are going well and I've got almost all my lines memorized. We're supposed to be off book by next week. I love being Belle! It's such a fun part. How's everything with Geoffrey? Is he still staying there? Are his termites gone?"

"Funny you should mention that. There was a problem with the termite tenting thing and now his house is flooded. Some of his furniture is ruined. And he has to replace the downstairs flooring. It's going to take a while to fix everything."

"He should move in with us!" Jalina said, without hesitation.

"Are you sure sweetie?"

"Yeah, of course."

"What a generous and loving heart you have. That's a wonderful gesture, thank you. I'm so proud of you that you want to open up our home to him."

"I really like him. And he makes you happy, so I'm happy for you. I'm all for it."

"Good, I was hoping you'd say that because I already told him he could stay with us. But we'll have to make a few changes. It won't just be us girls anymore."

"Like, what kind of changes?"

"Like, you can't walk around the house in your underwear anymore. And you'll have to sleep with your bedroom door closed."

"Mommy, please. I'm not gonna let him see me in my underwear," she giggled.

"Good. It wouldn't be appropriate. Is your dad there?"

"Yeah, do you wanna tell him, too?"

"I think I probably should."

"Okay, just a minute." She yelled, without covering the phone, "Daddy, Mommy's on the phone and she wants to talk to you."

"Bring me the phone then, dork," Tara heard him holler back. Then she heard muffled giggling. Joe must have put his hand over the phone.

"Hello?" Joe said expectantly.

"Hi, I have something to tell you."

"You're getting married."

"Not quite, but you're not too far off."

"I was being sarcastic."

"I know. But I'm not." Tara told him about Geoffrey's house crisis and the temporary move and he didn't like it.

"I think it's way too soon and you're rushing things. I'm curious though, what's Geoffrey's 'professional' opinion on the matter? What does a therapist think of this lunacy?"

"He said there is no magic formula for dating and getting to know one another in a relationship. He said that it should be based on the couple's intuition and how they feel about each other."

"I see. I guess that makes sense. Tara, I trust your judgment and know you have Jalina's best interest at heart. If you say he's a good guy and Jalina's cool with it, then I wish you both well. You have my blessing."

"Thank you, that means a lot to me."

"Have you told him about your depression yet?"

"No."

"You definitely need to tell him. That's a huge secret to keep from him, don't you think?"

"I hadn't thought about it. I'm not taking medication for it anymore and it's completely under control."

"It's your call, but I'd want to begin a new relationship with full honesty."

"You're right, I'll tell him."

They hung up and Tara had one more call to make. She was exhausted, but knew she needed to tell her mom. Kate took the news better than Tara thought she would. She said she was happy for them and wished she could meet Geoffrey.

Kate and her husband, Jack, resided in Portland, Oregon. She felt helpless being a thousand miles away from her only daughter and granddaughter. Even though she claimed to be happy, Tara sensed her underlying sadness and knew she felt left out. Tara promised they'd visit soon.

16

Dorey

TARA BRUSHED HER teeth and got ready for bed, longing to slip between the sheets and put this day behind her. The doorbell rang. She looked at her new watch, smiled, and shook her head. *What a crazy couple of days I've had.* It was nine-thirty but felt like midnight.

Tara jogged downstairs and peered through the little window in the door. Dorey's eyeball was peering right back at her. She opened the door.

"Well, hello, pretty lady, what's happenin'?" Dorey waltzed in, squeezed Tara and flopped down on the couch.

"I wouldn't know where to begin," Tara said. She watched Dorey and changed the subject. "How've you been? Where did you just get back from this time?"

"Uh uh, you're not getting off the hook that easy. Something's going on, I can tell. Hey, you cut your hair. It looks good."

"Thanks. Can I get you something to drink?"

"Hell, yes! Since when do I turn down a free glass of booze?"

"Good, I was hoping you'd say that. Geoffrey doesn't drink and I haven't had a drop since the last time I hung out on the porch with you a month ago. Gee, has it only been a month? Feels like years." Tara got out a bottle of wine and two wine glasses. She took them to the living room and poured generously.

"Hey, have you lost weight? You look skinny." Dorey lifted her glass and took a long drink.

"Thanks, I started working out again a couple weeks ago," Tara took a drink. "At first I was just doing exercises at home, but Geoffrey offered to train me. Yesterday, I got a gym membership and we worked out together. He gave me my own customized workout plan."

"Really? How'd that go?"

"Not great at first. He said I was weak. He also called me lazy and pathetic," Tara paused. "He apologized later and felt terrible for saying those things to me. Look, he even bought me this watch."

"Uh huh. Nice watch," Dorey said while barely looking at it. "That shit. What did you do?"

"He tried to explain why he gets so worked up over things. He told me his mom was really hard on him. She used to call him lazy, too. She insulted him all the time, and even abused him as a child."

"And then what happened?"

"I forgave him. We all have baggage."

"Of course you did," Dorey interrupted. "You know what your problem is, lady? You're too nice. You're just too good and too sweet and people take advantage of you."

"Here we go again. Haven't we had this conversation?"

"It obviously didn't do any good, so we're havin' it

again."

"I've struggled with conflict my whole life. I'd rather forgive, move on, and keep the peace, ya know?"

"No, I don't know. Explain it to me."

"Well, not everyone can be fiery like you."

"Like me."

"Yeah."

"So, tell me about this struggle with conflict."

"I'm just another cliché with daddy issues, that's all. Nothing to tell."

"What the hell are you talking about?"

"You know, how people, especially women, blame their fathers for their messed up relationships with men."

"Sucks to your ass-mar."

"My what?"

"Didn't you ever read *Lord of the Flies*?"

"Sure I did…back in high school. But what does that have to do with anything?"

"There's a line in it referring to Piggy's asthma…oh never mind. You know how I love to say weird shit.

Anyway…I don't have daddy issues. Not everyone does, you know. So, speak for yourself. My dad is the best dad in the universe. We have a fantastic relationship. And I'm still single. I don't blame him one bit. So stop projecting and tell me how you really feel."

"I can't"

"Yes, you can."

"I have abandonment issues because—"

"Don't give me labels. Tell me what happened."

Tara sighed and took a long drink of her wine keeping her eyes closed. She set the glass down and glanced at Dorey, who was waiting patiently. She cleared her throat and began her story.

"My parents divorced when I was two. My mom and I

moved out of state when I was four. I was shipped back and forth between Portland and Seattle, summers and school vacations, to spend time with my dad. But he never wanted to spend time with me. He'd send me to visit my grandparents, uncle, or even the neighbors. It seemed like he looked for ways to get me out of his hair.

"The few memories I have are fleeting images of my trying to please him or win his approval. I wanted some scrap of attention, like a flea-bitten stray dog begging for table scraps—crumbs.

"Nothing I did was good enough. If I got five A's and one B on my report card, he'd say, 'What's the B for? You didn't study hard enough.'

"I don't remember him complimenting me or hugging me, or even telling me he loved me. He was not an affectionate man. He was distant and critical. He seemed perpetually disappointed in me, like he was annoyed that I had even been born.

"We didn't have anything in common. His hobbies revolved around sports and I was un-athletic and awkward. He mentioned on more than one occasion that he'd wished I was a boy." Tara's eyes watered as she stopped talking, lost in the memories of her childhood.

"So, because you didn't receive love and affection from your father, you let men walk all over you?" Dorey asked.

"No! I don't—"

"Hey, don't get defensive," Dorey reached across the couch and put a hand on Tara's knee. "I'm just trying to help. I want to help you understand why you allow yourself to be mistreated."

"I told you. It's fear of abandonment. I don't want to be left again," Tara sniffed, fighting back tears.

"My dad left me…Trey left me…Joe left me…I cling to my relationships. Once I feel a connection with someone, I try to make it work. Loyal to a fault, that's me."

"Is your dad still alive?"

"Yes."

"But the way you're talking about him all in the past. I assumed he…"

"We're not close. But like I said, I'm loyal. I still send him cards on his birthday and call him on holidays. It's pretty one-sided, but I try."

"What about Geoffrey?"

"What about him?"

"Are you going to break up with him?"

"No," Tara laughed. "Why would I do that? He loves me. He says he wants to marry me. Jalina adores him. He's going to stay here while his house gets some work done on it. A pipe burst and there was a terrible flood, and—"

"Wait. He's staying here?"

"Yeah."

"When?"

"The moving truck arrives tomorrow around noon."

"What? Tara, are you crazy? He can't move in here."

"Why not?" Tara insisted. "Jalina's on board with it, she even suggested it. Joe says he trusts me and gave me his blessing. Can't you just be happy for me? You're overreacting. You don't even know him."

"But I met him. I'm the one who introduced you, remember?"

"And we thank you for that. He may be the best thing that has ever happened to me."

"No, I don't think so." Dorey drained her glass and filled it up again, speaking slowly. "I told you to sleep with him, not marry him; just have some fun. Remember? I didn't think you'd fall in love with the guy.

"Tara, he's bad news. He's a very attractive, self-centered ego maniac. During our speed date he went on and on about his accomplishments and how successful he is, not once stopping to ask about me, for the entire eight minutes. He couldn't stop talking about himself. To be honest, I thought he was a total player and am shocked he wants to commit. He must be using you."

"Using me for what? I'm not rich. He owns a house in Newport Beach. Why would he need to use me?"

"I don't know, but I don't have a good feeling about him. Have you been to his house?"

"Not exactly."

"What does that mean?"

"Well, he's shown me pictures of it, but no, I haven't been there."

"Don't you think that's odd? He has a mini-mansion on the beach but prefers to spend all his time here in your little condo?"

"He said he's going to sell it and buy something closer to Jalina's school, so we can be together."

"And that doesn't sound suspicious to you? After you've only known each other a month?"

"Geoffrey says, 'when you know, you know.' And there are plenty of people who get married after only knowing each other a few weeks, and stay married for life."

"Just be careful, okay? I'd hate to see anything happen to you…I know you see the good in people and want to believe they can be trusted. But the truth is, not everyone is as good as you. Don't be so naive, okay?"

"Um…"

"Just promise me you'll look out for yourself. And, if I were you, I'd drive by this house of his and see if you can figure out what he's hiding from you."

Tara squirmed uncomfortably and looked at her watch.

"Oh shit, it's late." Dorey drained her second glass. "We're not gonna solve this tonight, kiddo," she said as she stood up. "Now, come here and give me a hug so we can both get some sleep."

Dorey left and Tara had doubts, *Am I making a mistake?* Her head hurt and she couldn't think anymore. She shoved the thoughts aside and went upstairs to bed, needing to escape into dreamland.

17

Moving Day

GEOFFREY ARRIVED JUST before the movers and asked Tara to help him unpack his car. He was scowling, irritable, and rubbing his temple. On edge, he snapped at her, "Tara, why aren't you ready? You can't move in slippers. Go put on your tennis shoes—now."

Tara flushed and ran upstairs like a scolded child. She winced as she reached for her tennis shoes, every muscle screaming in pain from three days of intense workouts. She gave up and left the shoes on the floor so she wouldn't have to bend over. She forced her feet into them without retying the laces and stomped out of the room.

She headed back downstairs warily. *What's his problem? He didn't greet me at the door with a hug and kiss. He didn't greet me at all. He didn't even smile at me.* Unnerved, Tara had no idea what to attribute to Geoffrey's sour mood. She kept quiet and moved as quickly as she could, hoping it would soon blow over.

They got his car unloaded and moved out of the way just as the moving truck showed up. *Where's Geoffrey?*

"Geoffrey? The movers are here," Tara called into the house. When he didn't answer, she walked out to greet the movers as they got out of the truck. She explained that it was her boyfriend's stuff and he'd be right there to talk to them.

"Ma'am, if you could just point out where you want this stuff, we can start unloading."

"Okay, sure," Tara said uncertainly, wondering what happened to Geoffrey. "Well, let's start with the garage. You can put the boxes over here, by these shelves. We'll go through them later and…"

A loud, ominous scraping sound emanated from the dining room.

Tara and the two men walked out of the garage and around to the side yard by the sliding-glass door. They witnessed Geoffrey manhandle her solid oak, clawfoot dining table—by himself. They watched him, awestruck, as he carried it across the yard and over to the dumpster, nearly half a football field away.

If she hadn't seen it herself she never would have believed it. The table was massive and weighed 160 pounds. Yet, Geoffrey made it appear as though he were merely lugging a cumbersome thirty-pound beanbag. It was unbelievable. He showed super-human strength like Tara had never seen.

When he reached the dumpster, he put the table down, opened the dumpster lids, then hoisted the table up to his shoulders and tossed it in. Tara and the two movers stood there dumbfounded, mouths agape.

Geoffrey walked past them without a word, went into the house and brought out four dining chairs, tossing them in as well. Then he grabbed Tara's wrist and pulled her with him, while he said, "I need to talk to you."

She looked over her shoulder at the movers and said, "I'm so sorry. We'll be right back," then disappeared into the garage with Geoffrey.

"I asked you to do one thing. One thing!" He released Tara's wrist and paced around the garage. "Where the hell was my table supposed to go? Huh?"

Rubbing her wrist and nearly in tears, Tara said, "I put my table on Craigslist and someone called to buy it but they didn't show up. There wasn't enough time."

"Why didn't you clean out the garage? Where's my stuff supposed to go? You didn't make any room for me. Tara, you knew I was moving in today. You don't care. There's no room in your life for me. I'm hurt that you didn't put more of an effort into this. I was so excited for this move. Do you even want me here?"

"Yes!" Tara nearly sobbed. "I cleared out a whole closet in my room and dresser drawers, and drawers in the bathroom, and the entire spare room for you. Yes, I want you here. I'll clear the garage out better, I will…"

"Don't bother. I need to think. Tell the movers to unload the truck and leave. And don't touch my stuff."

Geoffrey grabbed his keys, stormed out of the garage, and jogged to his car. Revving the Acura's engine, he peeled out, and left a bewildered Tara with a truck full of his belongings, and movers demanding to know where to put everything.

Acting on autopilot and adrenaline, Tara managed to direct the movers where to put Geoffrey's things. He brought more than she thought he would. Based on their last conversation, she thought he'd only bring his office furniture, clothing, and a few personal items. But, as more boxes and furniture ended up in her garage and driveway, she wondered if this was everything he owned.

The movers finished up and needed to be paid. Geoffrey still wasn't back. Tara called him but he didn't answer so she gave the movers her credit card. *Where is he?* She had no idea what was happening.

When the movers left, Tara sat down on Geoffrey's shrink wrapped dining chair and put her head in her hands, trying to figure out what to do next. Seeing him carry her table like that and the way he acted before he left, scared her. She saw a side of him she hoped never to see again.

Her phone rang. It was Geoffrey. He said he was on his way back and apologized for leaving the way he did.

The call lasted twenty seconds. She was numb.

"Oh, Tara," he called in a sing song voice. "I'm home."

How could he joke at a time like this? Tara was still reeling from his turbulent exit three hours earlier. She got up and joined him in the garage. "Where did you go?"

"I went to my parents' house. I had to talk to my mom."

"Your mom? But why?"

"She calms me down when I'm upset. I'm sorry, I should have told you earlier. Moving stresses me out. I can't explain it but I have anxiety around moving. And then, when I got here and it seemed like nothing was ready, I just couldn't handle it."

"But, I did get the house ready for you. I did make room for your things."

"No. You didn't. And it still looks like you don't want me here. Everything is still shrink wrapped."

"You told me not to touch your stuff," Tara was incredulous. "I wasn't sure if it was staying or leaving again."

And then he lost it. "I'm done!" he yelled. "This was a bad idea. We're not a good match. I can't live with all this clutter. Why do you have so much stuff?"

He walked over to a shelf in the garage, pulled out a framed picture of Tara's grandparents and hurled it at the garage door. The glass shattered and the wood frame crumpled. "Why do you have pictures just laying around, unwrapped, unprotected? You must not care about what happens to them." He found another framed picture of her cousins, loose in a box. He took it out and taunted her with it.

"You're a hoarder. Nothing but a filthy hoarder. This garage is disgusting. Look at all this shit everywhere." He threw that picture, too, then tossed the box on the floor.

Tara stayed calm. Instinctively, she seemed to know that if she argued with him, or showed emotion, the situation would escalate and Geoffrey might become violent. The more upset he became, the calmer she became.

She knew he needed to get it out of his system. She had to let him carry on with his tantrum like an inconsolable two-year-old. She reminded herself this wasn't Geoffrey; this wasn't the man she loved.

"I want you to stay," she said in a clear, steady voice. "We can work this out and everything will be fine. Why don't we go in the house now and I'll show you your office?"

Geoffrey calmed down enough to go upstairs and look at the office Tara had put together for him. His desk, chair, book shelves, file cabinet, lamps, and even an easy chair were in the room. They were set up and the lamps had been plugged in.

"Thanks, I'll sleep in here tonight," was all he could manage.

Tara gave him a blow-up mattress to sleep on. He thanked her and assured her they'd talk in the morning and straighten things out. But she was too wound up to sleep. She went to the garage and organized her 'clutter.'

Tara spent the next five hours systematically unpacking, consolidating, and repacking her Christmas boxes, camping gear, paint supplies and tools. Both sides of the garage were lined with floor-to-ceiling metal shelving. She made use of every inch of every shelf, storing her things on top, and Geoffrey's on all the other shelves.

She made numerous trips to the dumpster, that is, another dumpster on the other side of the complex, and threw out a bunch of stuff. It felt good to purge the junk from her life. She wasn't a hoarder. She would show Geoffrey how neat, clean, and organized she could be.

Tara had done such a good job organizing the garage there was room for them to park both cars. She was pleased with herself and proud of all she had accomplished. She unwrapped Geoffrey's dining table and chairs before passing out from exhaustion at four in the morning.

After two hours of sleep, Tara was up again at six. She wanted to go to the grocery store because she was out of frozen berries for Geoffrey's morning protein shake.

Geoffrey woke up sad and embarrassed. He apologized to Tara with tears in his eyes. He was deeply moved when he saw the garage and even asked her, "How did you get those boxes up to the top shelf all by yourself?"

"It's surprising what a little adrenaline coursing through your veins can do," Tara winked.

Geoffrey grimaced and said, "I don't deserve you. How can I ever make this up to you? By the way, thank you for paying the movers. I'll pay you back along with the rent money I owe you. I just have to go to the bank first."

He took her in his arms and continued, "I love you, Tara. I'll never leave you. I'm looking forward to starting a life with you. I want to start our life together."

Tara was giddy and had to steady herself. It had been a

rocky twenty-four hours, and their first night together, as a cohabiting couple had been terrible. Yet, here she was, hopeful and in love again.

But she knew she couldn't tell anyone what had happened. They wouldn't understand. No one else saw this side of him. No one else knew the loving, gentle, affectionate, wonderful man holding her at this moment. The man who promised never to abandon her.

18

Everyone Needs Therapy

TARA WAS EAGER to make Geoffrey feel as at home in her house as possible. It was her last week day off. Work would start up again Monday and she wanted to be productive. She'd planned to hang up Geoffrey's art and pictures to surprise him. But he had a surprise for her instead. He said he didn't have any clients and had the day off.

They drank their morning shakes together, went to the gym, and came up with a plan to keep Tara on track. Geoffrey offered to take Jalina to school next week so Tara could hit the gym in the mornings before work. He'd only have to cover five days.

Jalina would be with Joe the following week, and the week after that was Christmas break and winter hiatus for Tara's job. *The Bad Wife* would resume filming the third week in January, giving everyone a month off for the holidays. With a clear plan in place, Tara was sure her fitness goals would be successful.

Plus, Geoffrey had her on a strict diet. Her current meal plan consisted of protein shakes with frozen berries, raw veggies, the occasional snack of almonds or a hard-boiled egg, and lots of salads, with lemon juice for dressing. The fat melted off and Tara trained hard.

After they unpacked Geoffrey's clothes together, selected which paintings he'd like to hang, and organized his office, Tara excused herself to chop veggies and prepare a chef salad for lunch. While she was in the kitchen, she heard the sound of nails being pounded into a wall. Curious, she went upstairs to investigate.

She walked into the office and saw Geoffrey admiring a samurai sword. It was sheathed in a black and gold case, with a jewel encrusted handle. It hung on the wall above his book shelf. "It's beautiful," she said.

"Yes, it is. Remember when I told you I had it? And that it's been passed down many generations?"

"I remember. It last belonged to your grandfather, right?"

"Yes, that's correct. But I didn't tell you the full story. My grandfather used it to end his life so he could die with dignity and honor. He had to die to restore honor to the family."

"I'm so sorry."

"Don't be. He believed he was doing the right thing. Hara-kiri was considered an honorable way to die among Japanese custom, especially when shame had befallen them for being put in an internment camp."

Since Tara had already heard the story from Wendy, she wasn't sure what to say. "Do you want to talk about it?"

"No, not right now. Is lunch ready? I'm starved."

"Almost. I just need to toss it and add the dressing."

They ate lunch at Geoffrey's table which looked brand

new. Tara was careful to put down place mats. "I love this table and, you're right, it looks great in here. How long have you had it?"

"I bought it two years ago when I mov—I mean, when my wife moved out and we got divorced."

"You don't talk much about her. What was she like?"

"No, I don't. I've told you everything you need to know. Besides, it's not healthy to ruminate about the past. The past is the past, let's leave it there. We need to be mindful of the present and hopeful for the future. I don't talk about my ex just like I prefer for you not to talk about yours."

"Exes."

"I beg your pardon?"

"You've been married twice, so that would be exes, plural."

"Thanks for the reminder. I'd appreciate a change of subject, if you don't mind."

"Sorry."

They ate in silence until Tara realized she hadn't told him Jalina's reaction to their living together yet. "I told Jalina, Joe, and my mom about our moving in together. You keep saying you're taking this seriously and are committed to our relationship. I want to show you I'm committed, too, and telling people makes it real."

"What did they say?"

"Jalina's happy for us. She really likes you. In fact, when I told her about your house being flooded, she suggested you move in with us before I could even mention it. I almost let her think it was her idea but I went ahead and told her the full plan so she'd be prepared by the time she comes back Sunday."

"That's great," Geoffrey smiled. "She's a good kid. I like her, too. What did your mom say?"

"She's happy for us, but feels bad that she lives so far away. She wishes she could meet you."

"We'll get a chance soon. Portland's not that far away," he chuckled. "Maybe we can fly up there some three-day weekend soon, like President's Day in February? Jalina will have that Monday off, right?"

"That would be awesome! Yes, we'll both have that day off. Mom would love that," Tara grinned. "What did your mom say when you told her?"

"She said she's happy for me, I mean us. She's looking forward to getting to know you better. And you'll get that chance at Christmas. She wanted me to invite you and Jalina to have Christmas dinner with our family."

"Thank you. I'd be honored. And I'm sure Jalina will love your nephews. She's great with little kids."

"I'm sure she is. The boys will love her. So, what did Joe say?"

"He thinks we're moving too fast. But he said he trusts my judgment and, if this is what I want, then he's happy for me."

"Do you think we're moving too fast?"

"Sometimes. But I'm glad we can talk it out, like now. I like that open, honest communication is important to you. And in that spirit, I have something I need to tell you." Tara's mouth went dry and her stomach did flip flops.

"What is it? You can tell me anything."

"In 2001, after the terrorist attacks of 9/11, I was diagnosed with clinical depression," Tara gulped. "I took anti-depressant medication for it and learned to manage it. And, after a few years I didn't need the medication anymore and was able to wean myself off."

"Is that all?" Geoffrey said with a laugh. "Why are you so nervous? I thought you were going to tell me something terrible."

"I thought maybe if you knew I had depression you'd look at me differently."

"Tara, I'm a therapist. Treating mental health patients is what I do for a living. You have a medical condition, that's all. The stigma our society attaches to mental health conditions infuriates me. Would you be embarrassed if you had to tell me you had diabetes? Or a heart condition?"

"No."

"It's the same thing. It's just that when things go wrong with the brain people don't understand it. The human brain is the least understood organ of the body. People attach negative energy to things they don't understand. Did you see a therapist?"

"No. I only went to a psychiatrist once. He diagnosed me and gave me the prescription. From then on I got my refills through my regular doctor."

"I think you would benefit from therapy."

"But, I don't feel depressed anymore."

"I know. But therapy is about more than just treating depression. Everyone has issues and, if you ask me, I think everyone needs therapy. It's a sick world we live in and people need to learn healthy coping mechanisms."

"Would you treat me?"

"No, of course not. Therapists don't treat their own friends and family. I can't treat someone I'm dating; I'm not objective enough. Besides, it's much easier to talk to a stranger. Maybe I can refer you to a colleague of mine."

"Okay…" Tara wavered, unconvinced.

In bed that night Geoffrey was attentive to Tara's every desire. It was like he was trying to right all his wrongs and make up to her for all the times he'd hurt her. He made love with his entire being, with an intensity and passion that consumed her.

She felt deeply connected to him and loved by him. Who was this enigmatic, moody man who had captured her heart? Perhaps because he was so passionate in the bedroom that passion somehow extended to other areas and caused his outbursts? *Ah, the many sides of my sweet, affectionate, tender, misunderstood lover.* Tara drifted into a peaceful slumber, still wrapped in Geoffrey's arms.

19

Crisis of Faith

TARA WOKE UP to see Geoffrey's beautiful, sleeping face inches from her own. She was still awed by his physical perfection and often wondered why he chose her. She smiled and caressed his cheek.

Geoffrey opened his eyes and grinned back at her, "I love waking up next to you and you having this big smile on your face. It's the best part of my day."

"I love waking up next to you, too," Tara beamed. "I know it happened fast, but I think our moving in together is a good thing. It gives us a chance to really get to know each other and I get to wake up next to you every morning. I can't wait to start the next chapter of our lives together. I feel so lucky right now."

"I love you, Tara. Those aren't just words to me. Every time I send you the heart symbol (<3) in a text, that's me shouting, 'I LOVE TARA!' That comes straight from my heart and I take it very seriously."

"I do, too, love you, and take it seriously," Tara squirmed. To recover, she climbed on top of him and wrapped her arms around him. "Let me show you…"

She covered him with kisses and they remained in bed for another hour.

On the drive back from the gym Geoffrey said, "Just because I'm in shape and work out regularly doesn't mean I don't have days when I don't feel motivated, too. I can't just be your trainer and coach. I need to be pushed, too. Let's help each other. Be a role model for me."

"Sorry, I didn't realize. You make it look so easy and you love to work out. I didn't think that you might need a push every now and then. I guess I got so caught up in you helping me that it didn't occur to me you needed help, too. You're the one who's inspiring me. You're the one who's making me a better person. To me, you're the role model."

"Tara, thank you, but that's a lot of pressure. Nobody's perfect, certainly not me, and I can't keep 'inspiring' you without getting some inspiration back. I need you to be strong for me. Can you do that?"

"Yes, I think so," Tara said quietly.

"That's my girl. We're a team. I'm training you, but you're learning and growing stronger every day. Take that knowledge and be my equal. Push me to be stronger, too."

"Okay," she smiled. But she didn't feel strong. She felt meek and didn't know how to push Geoffrey to work out harder. He already worked out harder than anyone she knew. How was *she* supposed to motivate *him*?

When they pulled into the garage Geoffrey nearly hit Dorey with the front of his car. She seemed to come out of nowhere and was standing in front of their garage. She darted out of the way and waved, then waited for them to get out of the car.

"Howdy, neighbors, what are y'all doin'?" Dorey said with an exaggerated southern drawl.

"Dorey, how nice to see you again," Geoffrey said.

"We just got back from working out at the gym," Tara said. "I did extra cardio and I'm exhausted."

"What do you do to stay in shape?" Geoffrey asked.

"I play tennis and I run," Dorey said.

"What kind of running? Marathons?"

"No, I travel too much with my job to train for something like that. But I squeeze it in when I can. Whether it's a run on a beach, treadmill in my hotel, or jog on some lovely wooded path, I just keep running. Besides, 'Just keep swimming' is way too goofy when your name is Dorey."

"That's funny," Tara said, laughing. "I loved that movie."

"I don't get it," Geoffrey said.

"You didn't watch *Finding Nemo*?" Tara asked.

"No, never heard of it."

"I guess that makes sense since you don't have kids. I thought maybe your step children would have had it. It's an animated film for kids but I know a lot of adults who love it too. Anyway, there's a character in it named Dory. She's a fish and she helps this other fish look for his missing son."

"Sounds amazing," Geoffrey rolled his eyes.

"I'm not explaining it very well. It's a great movie. Trust me."

"Anyway," Dorey cleared her throat. "Let's all go out to dinner tonight. Now that you two lovebirds are shackin' up, I want to get to know the man who stole this lovely lady's heart."

"Oh, no thank you, we—" Geoffrey protested.

"I insist. I won't take no for an answer. Besides, I'm paying so don't insult my good will effort at being a good neighbor."

"Since you put it that way how could we say no?" Geoffrey said.

"There ya go, good answer," Dorey winked. "I'll come over and pick you two up at six thirty. See ya then."

They showered, dressed, and Geoffrey had some paper work to go through in his office. Tara sat in the chair behind his desk, keeping him company. She spotted a photo album on his book shelf and pulled it out.

"What's this?" She opened the album to see a younger version of Geoffrey staring back at her in open, unzipped jeans and nothing else leaning against a cherry red sports car. "Whoa! That is seriously sexy. You were HOT! I mean, you still are, but—"

"Thank you," he chuckled. "That's my modeling portfolio. I was a fitness model in my twenties and early thirties. I mostly did magazine ads for 'Men's Health' and a few others."

"Why did you stop?"

"My agent didn't send me on enough jobs. She said she submitted my pictures, but it was just too competitive. Believe it or not, there are tons of guys out there who look like me."

"What? No way, man. You're the hottest of them all." Tara put the portfolio down and walked over to Geoffrey. She slid her arms around him from behind and nibbled his ear. "I am one lucky chica," she whispered.

Dorey took them to TAPS Fish House, an upscale seafood restaurant in Irvine. Tara was going to get a salad, but Geoffrey stopped her and said she was allowed a cheat meal.

"*Allowed* a cheat meal?" Dorey raised an eyebrow.

"Yeah, I'm on a diet, just until I lose a few more

pounds," Tara replied.

"You're a stick already, lady. You don't need to lose a thing," Dorey said.

"Tara's losing fat and building muscle. To do that, she has to shake things up a little. Her body is holding onto the stored fat so she has to modify her diet until her body sheds the fat."

"That's unhealthy," Dorey challenged.

"I assure you it's perfectly fine. There's nothing wrong with a caloric deficit once in a while. It's good for her. She's cleansing her body and removing toxins."

"You're starving her. Is she allowed any fats?"

"Of course. She's fine."

"Are you a certified nutritionist? Dietician?" Dorey shot back. Then to Tara, "Eat whatever you want tonight, honey." She leveled her gaze back at Geoffrey, "It's her body."

"Dorey, it's okay," Tara pleaded. "I want him to help me. I asked him to train me and part of training involves diet. I do have extra fat I want to get rid of. I want to be in better shape."

"I suppose she's not allowed a glass of wine either?" Dorey wouldn't let it go.

"She can drink whatever she wants. Like you said, it's her body," Geoffrey shot back.

"Great! Two glasses of Chardonnay, please. Unless, Geoffrey, do you want any?"

"I don't drink alcohol."

"That's what I thought."

The server took their orders and they sat in silence for a while.

Dorey broke the silence with, "Tara tells me you're a Buddhist. What does that entail? Do you go to Buddhist temples and pray?"

"I don't participate in the religious aspects of Buddhism. I practice what is referred to as Secular Buddhism. I study its philosophies and teachings."

"So, you don't pray?"

"No, I don't."

"Why not?"

"Because I don't believe there's a God. Buddha was not a god. He was a man, and therefore should not be worshipped."

"What do you believe in?"

"I believe that nothing is fixed or permanent and that change is always possible. Life is suffering. Everyone suffers. Desire and attachment are the causes of suffering. But with meditation and mindfulness we can ease suffering."

"Ladies, your wine," the server announced, and put two glasses on the table.

"Oh, thank God," Tara grabbed for her glass. Geoffrey and Dorey both stopped and stared at her. "Sorry, did I say that out loud?" she blushed, then took a sip of her wine.

Dorey clinked glasses with her, "Cheers!" She gave Tara a wink.

"Cheers," Tara glanced at Geoffrey, then took a long drink.

"So, Geoffrey, where were we?" Dorey continued her questioning. "Oh yeah, what's mindfulness?"

"Mindfulness is the state of becoming aware of ourselves in the present moment. We become aware of our bodies, feelings, and mind. Through constant vigilance in thought, speech and action, we seek to rid our minds of self-centered thoughts that separate us. By being aware of our thoughts, emotions, body, and world as they exist in the present moment our thoughts create our reality.

"I also practice meditation, which helps me train my

brain to focus on the here and now with more clarity. Deep meditation leads to a higher state of consciousness, with the goal being enlightenment."

"I see. So…if I'm mindful in the moment my present thoughts will create my reality?"

"Precisely."

"What if my thought is that I'm cold, but the reality is that it's eighty degrees in here?"

"It takes practice and mental discipline. Mindfulness is not simply mastered over one dinner."

"Touché."

Just then the server showed up with hot plates of delicious looking food. *Just in time,* Tara sighed. *Before they kill each other.*

After Tara thanked Dorey again for dinner and said goodnight she came inside to find Geoffrey sitting on the couch. "Why'd you get so quiet once the food arrived? It was like you didn't want to be there anymore and you didn't contribute to the conversation at all."

"I started getting a headache," Geoffrey replied. "Besides, you two girls needed to catch up."

"Why didn't you say anything?" Tara sat on the edge of the couch and touched his knee.

"I didn't want to ruin your evening with Dorey."

"How do you feel now? Do you want some Advil?"

"That'd be great, thanks," Geoffrey closed his eyes and pinched the bridge of his nose.

Tara got up to get the Advil and a glass of water for Geoffrey. She came back, gave him the water and pills, and dimmed the lamp next to the couch. She sat down on the chair next to the couch and thought about their pre-dinner conversation.

As if he could read her mind, Geoffrey said, "Tara, I

want you to stop going to church."

She had a feeling this was coming. He'd already showed her a few anti-religion documentaries and had been slowly wearing her down. They talked about mindfulness and Buddhist philosophies all the time. She looked up and met his eyes but said nothing.

Geoffrey continued, "You need to think for yourself. Don't be a sheep, a follower blinded by faith. The world is a bad place with evil conspiracy theories and a government that lies to us. Everyone in organized religion is corrupt. Churches are corrupt. So, why would 'God' answer our prayers?

"Bad things happen. Life is suffering. We have to deal with it and trust no one. But it's up to us to be mindful and positive and good anyway. Do you understand?"

"Yes, I think so," Tara managed.

"Let me put it like this. I want to get to know you better. Who is Tara? You're a good person. You care about others, do favors for people and you're very nice and sweet. But, do you do the right things? What kind of person are you really—when no one's looking? Are you honest and kind and good and noble?"

Tara didn't know what to say and she didn't want to argue with him. She was tired and sad and she just wanted to keep the peace. Against her own conscience she gave up something that had been important to her, her faith. She became a skeptic and quit going to church. She wanted so desperately to be loved and accepted she tried to change herself into the person Geoffrey thought she should be.

20

Keeping the Peace

TARA STAYED IN bed instead of getting up to go to church Sunday morning. She tried to be positive, reminding herself that she got to sleep in and would have extra time on Sundays. She looked forward to picking up Jalina later, as it was her week. She missed her daughter terribly but was wary of how the week would go now that Geoffrey lived there. And she dreaded having to tell Jalina about her decision not to attend church anymore knowing it would affect her too.

It was now December and the formerly once a week *Beauty and the Beast* rehearsals were in full-swing, every day after school, as the cast and crew prepared for opening night a mere month away. Between the gym and work for Tara, and school and play rehearsals for Jalina, it was a busy time.

Geoffrey helped with driving Jalina to school in the

mornings so Tara could go to the gym. And Jalina was in a carpool with other kids from the play so she had rides home from rehearsals. The week flew and Tara felt like she'd hardly seen either one of them even though it was Geoffrey's first full week of living with them.

In the evenings while Jalina did homework Geoffrey spent time in his office. Tara thought he was avoiding them, but he insisted he was not avoiding anyone. He said he just needed to catch up on paperwork from his client intakes.

The time Tara spent in the gym was paying off. Soon, her fat dissolved into lean muscle. Her waistline was shrinking and she was growing stronger—inside and out. She was gaining a confidence she didn't know she had.

Geoffrey noticed the changes and pushed Tara even harder toward perfection. He controlled every aspect of her appearance. He made sure she dressed in fashionable, form-fitting clothing, wore makeup the right way, bought root-touch up to apply in between hair appointments so a gray hair never showed, and even insisted she wear heels.

The makeup issue bothered her because she'd always preferred a more natural look. She felt attractive enough and believed real beauty came from within. When she brought it up, Geoffrey countered with, "Have you ever seen a geisha?"

"You mean the Japanese women who paint their faces white?"

"Yes. But it is more than that. Their makeup is art. Their faces are immaculate. Perfect. They appear to have a flawless, porcelain skin tone."

"You want me to wear white-face makeup?" Tara was incredulous.

"No, of course not."

Tara sighed with relief.

But Geoffrey continued, "You don't have to use white foundation, but I do want you to use a foundation. It evens out your skin tone and makes it smooth.

"Tara, you are a beautiful woman. With your features, high cheek bones, and stunning eyes you could look perfect. Don't you want to look perfect for me?"

It wasn't worth fighting over.

She went along with it because it was important to Geoffrey. And when things were going well he was affectionate and attentive. He complimented her and made her feel loved. She was eager to please him because she felt she'd made too many mistakes in her marriage to Joe. She was determined not to repeat them.

She knew she'd taken Joe for granted and didn't consider his needs enough. She hadn't shown him her appreciation often enough. By doing everything Geoffrey asked of her, she hoped she was showing him that she respected and appreciated him.

On her way home from work Thursday, Joe called her. Tara answered the phone with her hands-free Bluetooth built into the car, "Hello?"

"You gave up your faith for him?" Joe asked, his words tinged with sadness.

"Hi, Joe. How are you?" Tara replied, with a sigh.

"Tara, I'm worried about you. You didn't give up anything for me. Why is this guy so different?"

"Ouch. What makes you think I gave up my faith for him?"

"Jalina told me."

"Oh, right. Okay…I'm trying to do things differently this time around. I don't want to make the same mistakes I made with us. I want this to work. Relationships take compromise, right? I have to give it my all."

"Compromise or sacrifice? You're losing yourself. And

losing your own values and morals in the process."

"No I'm not, Joe. You don't understand. I know what I'm doing."

"Do you?"

"He loves me," Tara whispered. "And I don't want to lose him like I lost you."

Silence.

"Joe, I gotta go. I just pulled into the driveway and Geoffrey's here. Bye."

"Be careful Tar—"

She hung up before he could finish. She wanted to hear another lecture from her ex-husband like she wanted a root canal. She wasn't in the mood.

When Tara walked through the door, Jalina and Nala greeted her with hugs and slobbery kisses. Well, Nala's kisses anyway. "How're my two favorite girls?" she asked, patting them both on the head.

Jalina giggled and replied, "You're silly, Mommy. Nala doesn't know what you're saying."

"Really? Are you sure about that?"

They both looked at Nala as she sat next to them, tail wagging, watching their every move as if she followed their conversation.

Tara took off her shoes and hung up her jacket in the coat closet. "Where's Geoffrey?"

"He's upstairs in his office."

"Have you eaten?"

"No, I just started my homework. Skyler's mom dropped me off from rehearsal a few minutes ago."

"How about if I heat up the leftovers from last night?"

"Sounds good to me."

"Great, I'll do that and you go back to your homework." Tara went to the kitchen, and Jalina went back to her studies at the dining table.

Once she'd gotten dinner taken care of for Jalina, she excused herself and went upstairs to see if Geoffrey wanted any. She knocked on the door and waited.

"Come in," came Geoffrey's cheerful reply.

Tara opened the door, "Hi honey, I just got home and heated up some leftovers for Jalina. Are you hungry? Can I get you anything?"

"Oh, no thanks. I grabbed something on my way home earlier. But, have a seat, there's something I want to talk to you about."

Tara sat in the reclining chair behind Geoffrey's desk. He turned his chair around to face her and began, "I don't want you hanging out with Dorey anymore."

"What?"

"She's a bad influence on you."

"What are you talking about?"

"She came over about half an hour ago looking for you. It got me thinking about last Saturday night and our dinner with her. She's very pushy and at dinner she kept pressuring you to drink. I'm not comfortable around her. I don't like her and I would appreciate it if you stopped being friends with her."

"Wow, I'm sorry you feel that way. But, Dorey's been a great friend to me..."

"You have me now." He reached over and pulled Tara onto his lap giving her a passionate kiss. "Would you rather hang around with your single know-it-all friend who gives bad advice or me?"

Tara didn't want to have to choose between them. It wasn't fair. She knew they didn't like each other at the restaurant. There had been an air of tension all night. But she knew better than to argue and acquiesced to Geoffrey's wishes.

She'd recently read an article about women and

relationships. The article stated that the subconscious mind was created in the first seven years of life. It said that people's brains are in a hypnotic state during this period and everything in the environment is downloaded without filters. This includes the beliefs, attitudes, habits, and behaviors of the family.

Then the expert said, "We (women) have been conditioned to be nice, act happy, keep quiet, and keep the peace."

Tara didn't know how to operate any other way, and she didn't know how to change her programming.

21

Mission Tiki Drive-in

IT WAS SATURDAY and Tara's last night with Jalina before she went back to Joe's for a week. She wanted to do something fun that everyone would enjoy, to give Jalina and Geoffrey a chance to get to know each other better. She suggested they go out to dinner and a movie.

"Hey, weren't you telling me the other day about that old drive-in movie theater that's been redone?" Geoffrey asked. "I haven't been to a drive-in since I was in high school. We should find out what's playing tonight. What do you think?"

"Yeah, one of the moms at Jalina's rehearsal told me about it. It's called the Mission Tiki Drive-in and it has totem poles and a tiki-theme. And you don't have to put those bulky metal speakers on your window anymore. Now you just tune in the frequency on your car radio. Plus, Jalina's never been to a drive-in before."

"What's it like, Mommy?" Jalina asked.

"Well, when I was a kid I got to bring a friend and we'd go to the movies in our pajamas. We'd put the back seat down and load it up with pillows and blankets. It was always a double-feature. We'd watch the first movie with my parents, then crash during the second movie.

By the time we got home we were already ready for bed so we just sort of sleep-walked ourselves to bed. As hard as we tried, we couldn't seem to stay up late. But there was something thrilling about watching a movie outside in the dark, from the safety of our car. What do you think, Jalina?"

"That sounds cool!"

"Awesome. It'll be fun to introduce you to something I did as a kid. Sort of a blast from the past, ya know?"

"Uh huh. Can I wear my pajamas? Can I bring Skyler?"

"Sure, but why don't I see what's playing before you call her."

"Okay, I'm gonna go pick out what pj's I want to wear. I'm so excited!" Jalina squealed and ran up the stairs.

It turns out drive-ins still played double features. They saw *Race to Witch Mountain*, a kid's movie featuring Dwayne Johnson, followed by *Witness*, an older movie featuring Harrison Ford and Kelly McGillis. It wasn't a kid's movie but Tara figured by the time they showed *Witness* Jalina would be asleep.

They took Tara's car, a 2005 Toyota 4Runner, because Geoffrey's Acura didn't have a back seat. Since Skyler wasn't able to go Jalina brought Nala instead. When the action got tense, Jalina moved up to the center console in the front between Geoffrey and Tara.

Geoffrey rolled his eyes in annoyance when Jalina moved up front with them but covered it with a stretch and a yawn. He patted Jalina's knee and smiled at her.

Since *Race to Witch Mountain* was a fast-paced action movie, Jalina wasn't remotely tired when *Witness* started.

The movie was about a young Amish boy who witnessed a murder in a public restroom. Overall it wasn't scary but it had two violent scenes and mature thematic elements. Tara didn't think Jalina should be watching it and voted they call it a night and go home.

Geoffrey and Jalina both said she could handle it and Jalina begged to stay. Outvoted, Tara reluctantly let her daughter watch the movie.

When the movie ended Jalina had to go to the bathroom but was too scared to go by herself.

"I'll take her," Geoffrey offered.

"Thanks, honey," Tara said. "I'll clean up and pull the car around to meet you by the restrooms."

Jalina walked into the restroom and counted five stalls. She looked for feet and noticed all the stalls were empty. She was completely alone in the women's restroom. Geoffrey told her he'd wait for her outside but right now she was scared and wished her mom had come in with her instead.

"This is silly. There's no one in here. All I have to do is go in, pee, and come back out. There's nothing to be scared of," Jalina said to herself. Plus, her bladder was full from all the 7up she drank during the movies.

She sighed, went in the stall against the wall furthest from the door and pulled down her pajama bottoms and underwear.

Just as she had finished peeing and reached for the toilet paper, a hand suddenly reached under the stall next to her, grabbed her ankle and said, "Gotcha!"

Jalina screamed and jumped off the toilet seat so fast she almost went flying through the door with her pants still down.

Yanking up her bottoms, heart racing, hyperventilating and disoriented she ran out of the bathroom looking for her mom.

Geoffrey ran out of the stall after her calling her name.

She didn't stop running.

He caught up to her, grabbed her arm, and turned her around. "Hey, Jalina. It's me, Geoffrey. It's okay. It was just a joke. I'm sorry. Please, don't cry. It was a really lame and really bad joke. I had no idea you'd react like that. I was just having fun. I'm so sorry. Can you ever forgive me?"

Realizing her life wasn't in mortal danger and calming down a bit, Jalina sobbed, "Geoffrey, why did you do that? That wasn't funny!"

"I know. I'm sorry. I thought you'd know it was me and we'd both have a good laugh over my silly little prank. I was wrong."

Jalina's breathing slowed down and she sniffled then wiped her nose with her sleeve. She stopped crying and just stared at Geoffrey.

He gazed back at her then softly said, "Maybe it's best if you don't tell your mom about this, okay?"

"Why not?"

"Well, if you tell her that I scared you she might get mad and overreact. Then I won't get to show you a cool trick."

"What kind of trick?"

"Like, I know a special way you can fight off a bad guy so you never have to be scared again. I can show you how to defend yourself. Would you like to learn?"

Jalina sniffled again, then gave a slight nod.

"I'm a blackbelt in karate and I can show you a couple of really cool moves."

"Wow, like a ninja?"

"Are you saying that because I'm Japanese? Are you

making fun of me?"

"No, I wouldn't do that," Jalina said. "You're Japanese?"

"Half."

"That's so cool! But I mean a ninja warrior, like on *Kim Possible*. You know, people who are really good at martial arts and fighting."

"Ah, I see," Geoffrey stroked his chin. "Actually, ninjas are trained assassins and spies. Do you think I'm an assassin, Jalina?" He winked at her.

"No, silly, of course not. You'd never kill anybody."

"Right. Now that that's settled, want to learn those moves?"

"Yeah!"

"But you have to promise not to tell anyone. It'll be our little secret."

"I promise."

22

The Ring

TARA MADE CHOCOLATE chip pancakes for breakfast because they were Jalina's favorite. Also, it was Sunday morning and she felt guilty about not taking her daughter to church. While Jalina ate, Tara made a protein shake for herself. She was determined to lose a bit more weight even though her pants were getting baggy.

Her phone rang and she saw that it was Dorey. She ignored it. She knew she'd have to talk to Dorey eventually but she was dreading it and decided to put it off a little longer.

Geoffrey was in his office. He said he had paper work to do and didn't want to be disturbed.

Since Geoffrey was busy and Tara had Jalina until six when she'd have to drop her off at Joe's, she decided to make it a mother/daughter fun day. She loved spending time with Jalina and it had been a while since it was just the two of them.

This was the only day all week Jalina didn't have play rehearsals or something going on for school. Wednesday was the winter choir concert and Friday, the trimester awards assembly.

Tara took Jalina to a nail salon to get a manicure and pedicure. She figured a little pampering was in order to prepare for her big week.

After a fun afternoon with Jalina, Tara dropped her off a little early and headed home. She went upstairs to check if Geoffrey was still in his office. She saw the door closed and was about to knock when she heard him talking to someone on the phone.

She paused.

Something in his tone made her want to listen. *Okay, fine, eavesdrop.* Her skin prickled and her stomach clenched. *Was he flirting?*

Tara heard him tell his caller he'd been married before, and other personal details about himself. Then he laughed…that sweet, sexy 'I'm interested' laugh that Tara loved. He mentioned his sister lived nearby.

Tara had heard enough. She quickly knocked on the door and barged in without waiting for a response.

"Who are you talking to?" she demanded.

"My sister," he lied.

"You're lying to me. I want you out *now.*"

Tara slammed the door, stomped to her bedroom and slammed that door, then stared at it willing her body to stop shaking. The adrenaline coursed through her veins as she contemplated her next move. All she could think was *he lied to me* over and over. She caught him flirting on the phone with someone else and he looked her in the eye and brazenly lied to her.

Heart racing, mind a jumble, fight or flight instinct

kicking into hyperdrive, Tara ran downstairs and put on her tennis shoes to go to the gym. *That's a stupid idea. What am I doing? Why am I running away?*

She tiptoed back up the stairs and listened at Geoffrey's door. He was still on the phone. *Unbelievable.*

She heard him say, "I gotta get going, I want to get my gym workout in.... Are you busy later tonight? I look forward to—"

Tara ran downstairs again, not wanting to get caught eavesdropping. *Was he making plans to meet her?* Tara was in shock. This wasn't happening. She slowly climbed the stairs again and took a deep breath. His door opened.

She yelled, "What are you doing? Are you—"

"Tara, sit down," Geoffrey interrupted. He was calm. There was no emotion in his voice. He was the polar opposite to Tara at that moment. "Take a deep breath. Good. Now, hold it and let it out slowly."

"I'm not one of your patients. Don't tell me to calm down or try to control me," she snapped.

"If you don't calm down and get a hold of yourself we won't be able to have a rational conversation."

"I don't have time for rational. Are you having an affair? Are you cheating on me? What's going on?" she accused.

Geoffrey laughed. "Tara, how can I be having an affair when I'm here all the time?"

"Why did you lie about talking to your sister?"

"I did talk to my sister. I also talked to my mom and a friend from grad school. We were in the same program together and she's struggling to meet her hours."

"Her hours?"

"Never mind, it's not important. The point is, I've been on the phone a lot today. Why are you listening to my phone calls?"

Tara looked down at her feet and didn't say anything.

"Hmm, I wonder...are you going to hack into my computer next? Start reading my phone texts, too? I don't appreciate this invasion of my privacy, Tara."

Again, Tara said nothing. She just squirmed uncomfortably. Geoffrey went on.

"I have lots of female friends, mostly colleagues from school. Yes, the friend I was talking to just now is single but she's just a friend. I don't like this side of you, Tara. I'm scared and didn't know you could be so petty and jealous. Or that you trust me so little that you jump to these conclusions. I'm prepared to leave. I'll move out if that's what you want."

"No, of course that's not what I want," Tara said, somewhat in control of her trembling and fighting back tears. "But I'm sad and hurt and confused. I don't know what the truth is. I need time to think. I'm going to take Nala over to Joe's. I told Jalina I'd drop her off later since we didn't take her with us earlier. Then, I'm going to the gym. We'll talk when I get back."

While at the gym all Tara could think about was Geoffrey and their relationship. *Is this the end of us?* He could be so moody and cold. And he had a temper. But he was also sweet, kind, affectionate, funny...she remembered their first date and how he'd made her feel at ease right away and calmed her nerves. He had been so friendly and outgoing.

When he was at his best he made her feel special and loved. He was gentle, tender, and cuddly, always touching her with soft caresses or impromptu neck rubs, passionate kisses, and teasing flirtations. And the sex was incredible. He seemed to know her body better than she did.

He always had a mischievous twinkle in his eye. And that laugh. Tara loved his laugh and could never get tired of hearing it. She felt drawn to him, a powerful connection from the beginning.

But what if he is cheating on me?

And then she was hurt and angry all over again. *I should just kick him out right now and be done with it. He's not going to get away with this. What an asshole.*

And so it went. Tara grappled back and forth, still unsure what to do by the time she got back home.

Geoffrey was still in his office when Tara arrived. *Figures,* she thought, as she rolled her eyes. She took off her tennis shoes, then went upstairs to take a shower.

"Tara, will you come in here a minute?" Geoffrey called from his office when she got to the top of the stairs.

"I was about to take a shower," Tara protested.

"Please? We need to talk."

With a heavy sigh, Tara walked in Geoffrey's office and plopped down in his easy chair. She was still in her workout clothes, sweaty, hair in a ponytail, and smeared mascara under her eyes from crying earlier. She knew she must look a mess, and all she wanted was to take a shower. *Let's get this over with.*

"What?" she demanded.

"Remember when you asked me earlier if I was having an affair and I laughed?" Geoffrey asked, light and breezy.

"How could I forget?"

"You're gonna laugh in a minute, but—"

"I doubt it."

"Tara, just hear me out, okay?"

"Fine."

"You've mentioned a few times that you miss wearing a ring. You've said your hand feels naked and you just want something there. Well...I was going to save this for Christmas, but given our little misunderstanding this afternoon I want to give it to you now." He reached in his bottom desk drawer and pulled out a little black velvet box.

He handed it to Tara.

"What's this?" her voice faltered.

"I want to show you how committed I am to us. I know it's too soon to get engaged but I wanted to give you something. I want our first Christmas together to be memorable. I got you a promise ring. You know, it's a promise to get engaged and get married at some time in the future…when we're ready."

"You mean, like a pre-engagement ring?"

"Yes."

"Wow."

"Open it."

Tara opened the box and peered at the small white-gold band with a princess cut center of four small diamonds inside a diamond shaped setting. It was simple, yet stunning. She took it out and tried it on while Geoffrey watched her closely.

"It's beautiful…thank you." She stretched her hand out before her and gazed at the ring. "I love it."

"Are you sure it's okay?"

"Yes, it's perfect. It even fits! How did you know what size to get?"

"Um, about that." Geoffrey reached in his desk drawer again and pulled out Tara's engagement and wedding ring set from Joe. He laid it on the desk. "I took this into the jewelry store and had it sized."

"You went through my jewelry box?"

"I hope you don't mind. I needed to know what size ring to get. But I was looking for any ring. I didn't know you still had your wedding set. You know, it's bad luck to keep this when you've been divorced."

"What do you mean?"

"Because the marriage ended in divorce the ring holds bad energy. By keeping it you block yourself from a new successful relationship."

"But what if I'm saving it for Jalina, for sentimental reasons?"

"You want to give your daughter a ring with bad energy? You got divorced. That ring doesn't hold good energy when the marriage ended in divorce. Why would you want to keep it? You wouldn't want to give it to your daughter because then you'd jinx her future marriage by giving her a tainted ring."

"I never thought of it that way. Sort of like karma for a ring? What should I do with it then?"

"Sell it. The jeweler I went to said he'd buy it."

23

Winter Concert

TARA'S EYES DARTED back and forth between the new ring on her formerly naked finger, at the nine o'clock position on the steering wheel, and the traffic in front of her. Yesterday had been an emotionally draining day. She had nearly thrown Geoffrey out and ended the relationship. And now she was pre-engaged. *What does that even mean? How has my life changed so drastically in a few hours?* She was still reeling by all that transpired last night and wasn't sure how she felt about it.

Work was fun, but awkward. Everyone noticed the ring immediately, much to Tara's surprise. But it wasn't an engagement ring and it felt weird to say a promise ring at her age so she just said it was a gift from Geoffrey. She told no one of the 'promise' aspect of it. She told them he wanted to buy her a pretty ring for Christmas. She said he was too excited to wait and gave it to her early.

After work Tara stopped at Kay Jewelers where Geoffrey had bought her new ring. She showed the diamond buyer her engagement/wedding ring set from Joe and he agreed to buy it. It saddened her to give up the rings she'd worn fourteen years and the moment was bittersweet. There were many memories attached to the rings, both good and bad.

But her life with Joe was over now. That chapter was closed and she had moved on. She was getting a fresh start with a new ring, new possibilities for love, and a life with Geoffrey.

When Tara got home, she rushed in to tell Geoffrey about selling the rings but he was sick in bed and asked not to be disturbed. He cocooned himself and stayed in bed for the next two days. Unlike Jalina, who wanted to be fussed over and taken care of when she was ill, Geoffrey wanted to be left alone—completely. Which meant he kicked Tara out of her own room. She slept in Jalina's room, since Jalina was at her dad's.

Tara found out the hard way just how much she should have heeded his advice and left him alone the next night when she picked up his favorite sushi hoping to cheer him up.

Instead, she was greeted with, "You *brought* me sushi? Take-out sushi is never good. Sushi must only be eaten fresh at the restaurant, don't you know that? Sitting in a plastic container in your car? Gross. No way that's fresh. You should throw it out right now."

He coughed a couple times then added, "Why can't you leave me alone like I asked you to? I don't want you to take care of me at all. What I want is a plain bean burrito, which I can make myself, and to be left alone. For the thousandth time, when I'm sick I want to be alone." He added, "You never listen."

"I'm sorry. I just wanted to do something nice for you. I thought that since sushi is your favorite…I thought it would still be good. It was only in my car for five minutes. The sushi place I went to is just around the corner…. I'm sorry. Let me get this stuff out of your way and I'll make you a burrito."

She took the tray and plate of sushi downstairs to the kitchen, wrapped it up, and put it in the refrigerator. She quickly got out a can of refried beans, shredded cheese and a tortilla, and made a burrito.

When she brought Geoffrey the burrito she tried a new tactic. This time she said, "Your illness and suffering are caused by negative karma. Now that the negative karma is ripening in the form of your cold, it's not obscuring your mind anymore. You can be freed from it."

"Stop. Just stop. You don't know what you're talking about. Don't even bother trying to quote Buddha to me. You're botching it up. Now please leave." He ignored the burrito, turned away from her, and pulled the covers up over his head.

Tara stood with her hand on the door and watched him, torn.

"Why are you still here?"

"Sorry." She backed out and closed the door, shaking her head.

With Geoffrey's psychology background he was infuriating to argue with. He turned her words around on her and made her sound like an idiot. She hated it when he was moody like this and reminded herself that it wasn't personal. He just needed time to himself when he was sick.

When Tara got home from work Wednesday Geoffrey was still sick and didn't want to go to Jalina's winter choir concert. Tara rushed to Jalina's school alone. Since the girls needed to arrive an hour early Skyler's mom had already dropped them off.

Tara arrived with two minutes to spare. Naturally, all the good seats were taken. Then she spotted Dorey waving her over. Her heart sank. She was surprised to see her at first but then realized she shouldn't be. Dorey hadn't missed one of Jalina's performances since they'd become neighbors a few months earlier. She adored Jalina. She even claimed to be Jalina's doting aunt since she didn't have kids of her own.

"Hey, pretty lady. I saved you a seat," Dorey winked at her.

Tara felt awkward but sat down next to her, hoping they wouldn't talk.

The choir came out and took their places on the risers. Jalina stepped forward, up to the microphone, and sang like an angel. Leading the choir in a beautiful rendition of "Gloria in Excelsis Deo (Angels We Have Heard on High)," she had the audience enraptured. She was a natural performer and all eyes were on her.

After the choir performed, it was the band's turn. Dorey tapped Tara's shoulder and said, "We need to talk." She motioned for Tara to follow her outside. Tara dreaded what was about to come.

Once outside, Dorey crossed her arms and gave Tara a stern look. "Okay, tell it to me straight. I can take it. Why have you been avoiding me? Spill it."

"I haven't been avoiding you, Dorey. I've just been really busy."

"Bullshit. You're a terrible liar, Tara. Come on, it's me."

"I'm sorry. I really have been busy. I only have two days of work left and then we have a month off. *The Bad Wife* is taking a mid-season winter hiatus. Things have been kind of hectic as we make sure the kids finish shooting all their scenes in time to wrap up before the break. I've also had to make arrangements with their schools to get their end of semester testing and final projects done. And with Christmas being next week I haven't even had a chance to get my shopping done."

"You could've told me that on the phone. Tara, I'm not stupid. You haven't returned any of my calls."

"I know. I have a lot going on right now. Maybe we should take a break for a while?"

"You're breaking up with me?" Dorey laughed. "Are you shitting me?" She crossed her arms and looked at Tara. "Ah. I get it. It's Geoffrey. Mutherfucker. He told you we can't be friends anymore, didn't he?"

Tara squirmed and looked at the ground.

"I knew it. He feels threatened by me. Ever since that disaster of a dinner over a week ago I had a feeling he'd try to get rid of me."

"I'm sorry, Dorey. He just doesn't know you like I do. He'll come around. Let's give him a little time, okay?"

"I sure hope you know what you're doing, hon. I won't call you anymore or make trouble for you with Geoffrey, if that's what you want. But I'll always be your friend. You can't get rid of me that easily. Now come here and give me a hug, pretty lady."

As they hugged, Tara blinked back tears and whispered, "I'll always be your friend too."

24

Tuna Casserole

BY FRIDAY, GEOFFREY felt much better. He even went to Jalina's school with Tara to attend the Fall Trimester Awards Assembly. Jalina won an award for outstanding student in English Language Arts and another one for Choir. She was surprised and happy to see her mom and Geoffrey there. Since it was the middle of the school day, she didn't think anyone would be there for her. She ate up the attention.

While Jalina was at play rehearsal after school, Joe called and asked if Tara would take Jalina home even though it was still his week. He had a date and it was too short notice to get a sitter.

"Joe, you don't need to get a sitter. Call me anytime. It doesn't matter to me if it's not my week. I love spending time with my daughter."

"*Our* daughter," Joe corrected. "I just thought with

Geoffrey there that you'd want some alone time with your boyfriend."

"Geoffrey and I get plenty of alone time. He'll be fine."

"Oh? Trouble in paradise?"

"Knock it off. I'll take her, it's not a problem." Tara hung up before he could say anything else. She didn't know why she still let him get under her skin like that.

After dinner, Geoffrey and Tara played a strategy board game called Blokus with Jalina. Each player stakes their claim and protects their territory by fitting as many of their pieces on the board as possible while strategically blocking their opponents.

It warmed Tara's heart to see Geoffrey making an effort with her daughter. He had Jalina giggling the entire evening.

When Tara tucked Jalina and Nala in for the night, Jalina seemed troubled by something.

"Sweetie, is something bothering you?"

"No."

"Are you sure? You know you can tell me anything, right?"

"Uh huh."

"Okay, then. Good night, sweetheart. I love you." Tara kissed Jalina's forehead and turned out her lamp.

"Mommy?"

"Yes, sweetie?"

"Is Geoffrey going to stay with us forever? Are you two going to get married?"

"Do you want us to?"

"I do, but only if you want to. I mean, he's really nice and I like him a lot. But I mostly want you to be happy."

"Honey, just having you for my daughter makes me happy. How'd I get so lucky to have the sweetest, most wonderfullest daughter in the world?"

"That's not a word," Jalina giggled.

"No, you're right. I was being silly. But Jalina, I want you to be happy too. You'd tell me if Geoffrey ever did anything that upset you or made you uncomfortable, wouldn't you?"

"Mhmm," Jalina squirmed. "I'm tired. Can I go to sleep now?"

"Of course. Good night, sweetie."

"Good night."

Tara closed the door and went down the hall to her own room. Geoffrey was already in bed, sitting up and watching a documentary about Buddhism on TV.

"How's Jalina?" he asked, when Tara finished brushing her teeth.

"She's good. She really likes you."

"I really like her, too. Now come here so I can show you how much I like her mom."

"Look who's feeling better," Tara teased.

She turned out the light and slipped into bed.

The next morning, Geoffrey and Tara dropped off Jalina and Nala back at Joe's, then headed to the gym. After they got a good workout in the rest of the day consisted of running errands, getting groceries, and Christmas shopping.

Geoffrey was actually fun to shop with, much to Tara's surprise. The crowds didn't seem to bother him and he kept up a cheery disposition all day. When a crazed shopper cut him off in line, he made up a funny story about her mental instability, claiming she was an escaped lunatic from the psych ward at the Loony Bin Asylum. He had Tara laughing so hard people moved out of her way— as though *she* were the crazy one.

Cozy and cuddled up on the couch next to her man

watching *It's A Wonderful Life*, after all their shopping and errands that day, Tara savored the moment. It was Saturday night and she was exactly where she wanted to be, in the arms of the man who loved her.

Tara got up early the next morning to clean house and wrap presents. With Christmas only five days away she wanted to make sure she had everything ready in time. Geoffrey stayed in his office most of the day and Tara hoped he wasn't in one of his moods.

Since it was cheat day, she decided to make his favorite comfort food for dinner. They usually shared one cheat meal a week. And Tara wanted it to be good.

Geoffrey had raved about his mother's tuna casserole and Tara got the recipe from her. She couldn't wait to surprise Geoffrey with it.

Joe dropped off Jalina and Nala at the usual time, six o'clock Sunday evening, and Tara called upstairs to let Geoffrey know dinner was nearly ready.

"Tara, what's that smell? What are you making?" Geoffrey asked, as he nosed into the kitchen.

"Can't you guess?" She teased. "Sit down at the table, I'll bring it out to you."

Jalina was already seated and waiting patiently when Geoffrey sat down next to her. "Hi, Geoffrey. You're gonna love what Mom made for us."

"Oh? Do you know something I don't?"

"Yep! But it's a surprise."

"Hmm, I see. I guess we better not ruin the surprise then. So tell me, how are play rehearsals going?"

"Mostly good. But some of the kids don't have their lines down yet and we open in less than three weeks. I'm really nervous. I've never had the main lead before."

"You'll be fine. Sometimes I hear you practicing your lines or songs in your room. You have a very good voice,

Jalina; a real talent."

"Thank you!" Jalina's face lit up.

"Dinner is served," Tara announced, as she brought out two plates of casserole, set them on the table, then went back for the third plate.

"Tara, is this tuna casserole?" Geoffrey asked.

"Not just any tuna casserole…"

"What do you mean?"

"Taste it."

"Tara, what did you do?" Geoffrey's brows furrowed as he cut into the meal with his fork and sniffed it, hesitant. He slowly took a bite and chewed excessively before he swallowed.

Tara held her breath as she waited.

"Mmmm, it's delicious! Geoffrey, don't you think it's delicious? Does it taste just like your mom's?" Jalina asked.

"Tara, where did you get this recipe?" Geoffrey demanded.

"I called your mom and asked her for it. She was very happy to—"

"Don't you ever call my mother without my knowledge. How did you even get her number?"

"Excuse me? Geoffrey, she was flattered. She emailed me the recipe, it wasn't a big deal."

"Where did you get her number?"

"Wendy gave it to me."

"You called Wendy, too? What the hell? Are you talking to my family about me behind my back?"

"No. It's nothing like that. Geoffrey, I called them for you. I wanted to surprise you. You've mentioned how much you miss your mom's tuna casserole and I wanted to make it for you. I thought you'd be happy."

"I don't like surprises."

"Clearly. I'm sorry I called your mother without your

permission. I promise to never bother her again."

"Tara, you don't understand."

"Enlighten me."

"Remember what we talked about before? About my upbringing?" He glanced at Jalina, then back at Tara.

Recalling their conversation about his abusive childhood Tara paled. She closed her eyes and winced, "I'm an idiot."

"I'll be hearing about this later. The casserole is excellent, by the way."

"Geoffrey, I am so sorry. I didn't mean to cause any trouble between you and your mom. I just—"

"I know. It's okay. I'll handle it."

"What's wrong?" Jalina asked. "Why would his mom be mad at him because you called her?"

"I forgot that she doesn't like to talk on the phone. She's shy and—"

"Tara, I think you've said enough."

"Right. Come on, Jalina. Help me clear the table."

25

The Office

EVEN THOUGH SHE had *Beauty and the Beast* rehearsals all day Monday through Wednesday, Jalina was happy to be on Christmas break. She loved rehearsing for the play which was nothing like being at school. She began counting down the days until opening night, hoping she wouldn't mess up such a big part.

Tara looked forward to some much needed relaxation and was glad to have a month off. She'd consistently gone to the gym for twenty-one days and the soreness had finally subsided. Unknown to Geoffrey, she'd been using ice packs at work. Plus, the set medic gave her a few massages during lunch to alleviate the muscle tension.

She didn't want Geoffrey to call her a wimp and knew he wouldn't approve. He despised weakness. But Tara had a very low pain threshold and seized every opportunity she could to get over the soreness as quickly as possible sometimes cursing herself for being so weak.

Geoffrey didn't have any clients Monday so they went to the gym together after Tara took Jalina to rehearsal. They had a late lunch at Yard House, then headed over to the theater to pick up Jalina and Skyler. Now that Tara had some time off it was her turn for carpools.

When Tara drove up to the parking garage cars were lined up at the red curb by the entrance. They were blocking traffic which caused Tara's 4Runner to stick out on the street with another car behind her.

"This is dangerous," Geoffrey commented. "Someone should say something."

Next thing Tara knew he got out of the car and walked up to the first car at the red curb. He asked the driver to move her car, a Suburban, and park in the garage which had plenty of parking spaces. He informed her that people couldn't get around her vehicle and were stuck out in the street. She was cool about it and moved. Then everyone else moved, and Tara was able to get into the parking garage and park.

Tara feared Geoffrey would yell at the other parent or insult her and make a scene. Her palms were sweating all over the steering wheel and her breathing was shallow as she imagined the other moms' judgmental stares.

But when Geoffrey got back in the car and told her what happened, everything was fine. He was calm and rational and Tara realized she'd been practically hyperventilating. "Tara, are you okay? Why are you looking at me like that?"

"I'm sorry. It's just that I thought you might be angry. I didn't want you to yell at that other mom and I was worried you might—"

"You thought I'd make a scene. Really, Tara? You thought I'd get all hot-headed? Over that?… Obviously you don't know me very well."

"Sorry. I should have given you more credit than that."

"Yes. You should have."

Jalina and Skyler ran up to the car and jumped in the back seat. "Hi, Mommy. Hi, Geoffrey. May I hang out at Skyler's for a while?"

"Sure, I don't see why not. How was rehearsal?"

"It was great!" both girls said in unison.

Tara drove them to Skyler's and dropped them off while Geoffrey sat in silence. She wondered why she had feared the worst. She thought it may have stemmed from watching her dad blow up in public as a child. He'd often yelled at waitstaff and others in customer service when things didn't go the way he thought they should. Perhaps Tara was projecting those memories onto Geoffrey. *Great. I've been hanging around a therapist too long. Now I'm psychoanalyzing myself.* She smiled at the thought.

When they got home, Geoffrey headed straight for his office. Tara sighed. She looked at Nala and said, "Well, girl, I guess it's just you and me tonight, huh?"

Nala pricked her ears, wagged her tail, and headed to the front door.

"Oh, you poor thing. You need to go out, huh? Come on, let's go on a quick walk. Geoffrey won't even know we're gone."

But when she returned five minutes later, Geoffrey was yelling. His big, booming voice called down the stairs, "Tara, get up here! And bring that *dog* with you."

"Uh oh, Nala, what did you do? Come on, let's go face the music."

Tara walked upstairs and into Geoffrey's office with Nala trailing behind her. Her ears and tail were down and she stayed behind Tara. Before Tara had a chance to take in the scene Geoffrey grabbed Nala and dragged her to a chewed-up book on the floor.

There were other papers and books strewn about but only one had been damaged. He pushed her nose into the book then hit her while saying, "Nooo! Bad girl!"

Then, just before releasing her, he kicked her hind-quarters and told her to "Get out."

Nala yelped and ran downstairs, cowering.

It was all Tara could do not to lose it. "Don't you ever hit my dog again. Is this how you treat her when no one's looking? No wonder she hasn't warmed up to you. She's terrified of you."

"Make her stay out of my stuff. She needs to learn a lesson."

"Maybe you should keep your door closed."

"I usually do."

"She's never chewed up anything of mine or Jalina's."

"She's a stupid, spoiled dog. She needs to learn some damn manners."

"You need to learn some manners," Tara said under her breath as she went downstairs to check on Nala.

She found Nala in her dog bed in the living room with her nose in the corner of the wall as if Nala had put herself in a time-out. She ran to the dog and threw her arms around her.

"I'm so sorry, sweet girl. You don't deserve this. I know it's been hard for you to get used to the new rules and adjusting to things with Geoffrey here, having to stay off the couch, and out of my bedroom. I know you don't understand. I love you and I'm going to make sure he doesn't hurt you ever again."

"Tara?" Geoffrey was standing behind her.

"Stay away from her."

"I want to apologize."

"I don't want to talk to you right now."

"Tara, I'm sorry. I know you're upset but—"

"Upset? I'm not upset. I'm livid! If you ever touch my dog again…"

"Tara, you're shaking. Let me comfort you." He reached out to her and she cringed. "Are you afraid of me? Do you think I'll hurt you? Oh my god, what have I done?"

Geoffrey sat down on the couch and held his head in his hands. His shoulders shook and Tara realized he was weeping, soundlessly. She had never seen him cry before and was at a loss.

She stood up and walked over to the couch. Without a word Tara sat down next to Geoffrey and put her arm around him. He leaned into her at first, then stiffened. He moved away a few inches and wiped his eyes before looking at her.

"Tara, I have something I need to tell you."

"I'm here."

"I haven't been completely forthcoming with you about my work situation."

"I've noticed you haven't had many clients lately. Didn't you say there's a lull in the office this time of year?"

"Yes and no. You see, my practice is still getting off the ground. I haven't had my license to practice therapy very long and haven't built up a clientele yet. The few clients I've had have been referrals sent to me by the other therapist in the office."

"Other therapist? I thought you said you have a private practice?"

"Yes, but leasing office space is expensive. My mom has a therapist friend who agreed to sublet her office to me when she doesn't have appointments. I have to work around her schedule but I haven't had enough clients for that to be an issue yet.

"I thought I'd have a steady client load by now. The lack of work has been very stressful for me and not at all where

I thought I'd be by now. Honestly, I haven't made enough money to break even…I've been living off my savings…and the money's almost gone."

"Is that why you still haven't paid rent or reimbursed me for the movers? Geoffrey, you've been here almost a month."

"I know. I'll get the money to you, I promise." He paused. "Tara, I'm so sorry for what I did to Nala. I didn't mean to take it out on her. But when I saw the mess she made in my office…no, that's an excuse. I haven't been myself lately. I'm so sorry. Can you ever forgive me?"

Tara's mind reeled with this new information. *He's unemployed? Broke? Has been lying to me? Am I being played? What about his house in Newport Beach?*

"I need a minute."

"Of course. I understand."

"Do you? You just told me you've been lying to me the whole time we've known each other, you hit my dog…and you 'understand?'"

"I haven't lied to you, Tara. I just didn't tell you everything. I am a licensed therapist and I will have a thriving business one day. It is just taking longer than I expected, that's all."

"What do you do all day? When you're supposed to be at your 'office?'"

"I've been working my butt off trying to drum up business, that's what I've been doing. I'm not going to sit here and account for every minute of my days. Either you trust me or you don't. The reason I'm even telling you this is because I'm trying to be transparent and candid with you, Tara."

"Okay, okay. Thank you for your candor. I know this isn't easy for you and I appreciate it. I have faith in you, Geoffrey. If you say you'll have clients soon, you will. I believe you."

26

So This is Christmas

CHRISTMAS EVE MORNING, Tara made pancakes for Jalina then took her and Nala to Joe's. It was their first Christmas after the divorce and they wanted to make it as normal as possible for Jalina. They agreed that Joe would spend Christmas Eve with their daughter and Tara would get her Christmas Day. It wasn't ideal but Tara was glad they had an amicable arrangement and that Jalina was able to spend the holidays with both parents. Even if not all together.

Geoffrey was in his office when Tara got home. She went upstairs and knocked softly on the door, "Geoffrey?"

"Come in." Tara opened the door to see Geoffrey sitting at his desk in workout clothes.

"Are you about to head to the gym?"

"Actually, I just got back. Have a seat, Tara. There's something I want to talk to you about."

"Okay…," Tara hesitated before sitting down on the

edge of the easy chair, not feeling prepared for what was about to come.

"How would you feel about getting engaged?"

"To be married?"

"Is there another kind?"

"Um…"

Geoffrey ignored the shocked look on Tara's face and continued, "It seems silly to use your new ring as a promise ring at our age and then get another ring later. What if we got engaged now but kept it between you and I, and then announced it officially in six months or so?"

"A secret engagement?"

"For now, yes. Let's let our families get used to the idea of us being together for a while before we spring it on them. Don't you think that's wise? But we can start planning the ceremony now, if you like…. What would you think of a destination wedding? I think it would be fun to get married on the beach, don't you?"

"The beach sounds—"

"Mexico, or Hawaii…oh, there's lots of great locations in the Caribbean, too. And I know a wedding photographer, good friend of mine. He'd give us a terrific deal. And, of course, we have to plan a honeymoon. Where in the world do you want to go? Where's your dream honeymoon spot, Tara?"

"I've always wanted to go to—"

"What do you say? Do you want to become Mrs. Tara Jensen?"

"Yes. Yes! Oh my gosh, I can't believe this is happening!" Tara sprang up and jumped into Geoffrey's arms. She smothered him with kisses, so elated she couldn't think straight.

"Tara, darling. Remember, not a word to anyone just yet, okay? All this planning and daydreaming is fun, but we're getting a bit ahead of ourselves."

"Of course," Tara agreed readily, lightheaded and lighthearted. Idealistic and romantic, Tara had forgotten any concerns she'd had about Geoffrey. He said he wanted to spend his life with her. And at that moment, that was all that mattered.

"Merry Christmas!" Tara rolled over in bed and planted a big kiss on Geoffrey. She was as excited as a kid. She loved holidays and Christmas was her favorite. There was just something about the magic of the season. "What time do we need to be at your parents' house?"

"What time is it?" Geoffrey's voice croaked as he opened one eye.

"Seven."

"Go back to sleep. We still have five hours. They're not expecting us until noon. Why are you in such a good mood, anyway?"

"It's Christmas!"

"Ugh."

"What's the matter? Don't you like Christmas?"

"No, I don't. I dread it every year."

"But, why? Who doesn't like Christmas? Who are you, Scrooge?"

"It's too commercialized and stressful. Emphasis is placed on the acquisition of presents and material goods. Plus, it is a religious holiday celebrating the birth of Jesus, and I don't believe in celebrating the birth of a man who died two thousand years ago.

"It's also a very lonely and depressing time of year for many people. In my field, it's very busy with new clients seeking therapy. But that is just a reminder to me that I don't have many clients."

"Mood killer," Tara joked. "I'm gonna jump in the

shower then go get Jalina."

"And I'm going back to sleep. I didn't sleep well at all last night. I'm very stressed about my lack of clients. Telling you about it only makes me feel better in that I can talk to you about it now. I'm exhausted. Good night."

When Tara knocked at the door at Joe's, he answered.

"Merry Christmas, Joe!" Tara nearly shouted.

"Merry Christmas, Tara. My, aren't you in a good mood. What gives?"

"Geoffrey asked me to marry him last night! Can you believe it?"

"Really? Wow...I'm not sure what to say."

"Oh, you don't have to say anything. Actually, pretend I didn't tell you," her hand flew up to her mouth. "Um, I shouldn't have told you. We're not telling people yet. It will be a while before we set a date. Please don't say anything to Jalina yet either, okay? Me and my big mouth."

"Relax. What wedding?"

"Thank you."

"Jalina, your mom's here..."

While Geoffrey slept in Tara and Jalina had their little Christmas with each other. They opened packages from their long-distance family members then called and thanked them for the gifts and wished them a Merry Christmas.

This was the first year in a while they didn't celebrate with Tara's family. And even though they enjoyed the quality mother/daughter time together, they admitted it wasn't as festive as a room full of loved ones.

Geoffrey came downstairs at eleven having showered and dressed. "Hi, Jalina. How are you? Are you ready to meet my family?"

"Hi, Geoffrey. Merry Christmas! I can't wait to meet

everybody, especially your nephews."

"You know they're just little kids, right? Liam is six, and Zak is only three. I'm worried you'll be bored."

"I love playing with little kids. I'm almost old enough to babysit."

"Is that right? Well, okay then. Shall we go?"

"Let me powder my face real quick and grab my lipstick," Tara said.

"Mommy, you already look beautiful."

"Thanks, sweetie."

"Go ahead, we have time," Geoffrey looked at his watch. Ten minutes later they were in Tara's 4Runner with Geoffrey at the wheel. He drove the short distance to his parents' house in Garden Grove. His family didn't participate in exchanging gifts except for the boys. Everyone bought something for Liam and Zak. And Erica made sure there was a token present for Jalina as well.

While Jalina played dump trucks on the floor with Zak, Liam read a book to Uncle Geoffrey. Tara helped Erica and Wendy in the kitchen and exchanged smiles with Wendy when they heard Jalina and Zak giggling.

"Well, aren't they two peas in a pod?" Erica said. "What? That's how you say it, right?"

"Right," Tara chuckled. "Like peanut butter and jelly."

"No. I don't like peanut butter," Erica took on a serious tone.

"Mom, it's just a saying. You don't have to like peanut butter. Tara agreed with you that the kids are getting along," Wendy explained.

"Can't you say something else then?" Erica asked.

"Bread and butter?" Tara guessed.

"Perfect. I like that. The kids are bread and butter."

Everyone laughed.

Christmas dinner consisted of a blend of Asian and

American cuisines. It wasn't the traditional ham dinner Tara and Jalina were used to but it was still delicious. After dinner, Erica took the kids out back to show them her garden. Liam liked helping her with it and had his own gloves and a few plastic gardening tools.

"Jalina fits right in here. She looks like she's having a great time," Wendy mused, as she and Tara cleared the table.

"She is. I can tell she likes your boys a lot. They're so sweet," Tara replied.

"My boys? Ha. They can be a handful but Jalina's great with them. She's a natural."

"Thanks," Tara began rinsing off the dishes. "Wendy?"

"Yes, Tara?"

"Why does your mom go by Erica?"

"Her given name is Eriko. She got tired of correcting people when the mispronounced it. Erica is just the American version. Her family still calls her Eriko and that's still her legal name."

"That makes sense."

"Hey," Wendy looked around. Her dad, husband, and Geoffrey went to the living room to watch a game. "Did you ever say anything to Geoffrey about the talk we had at Thanksgiving?"

"No, why?"

"I don't know. He seems kind of moody lately and he hasn't called me in a while. I thought he might be mad at me. You know, because I told you so much about our family, and my grandfather."

"I didn't say anything. Actually, he told me about your grandfather himself."

"He did?"

"Yeah. When he showed me his samurai sword he told me the story."

"Wow, I'm speechless. He doesn't usually reveal the family secrets to anyone. You must have quite an effect on him."

Tara smiled. "It makes me feel good that he can talk to me. But I get the feeling sometimes that he's holding back, hiding something."

"Like what?"

"I don't know. It's hard to explain but whenever I bring up certain topics he changes the subject immediately or distracts me."

"Hmm, my brother is sort of an enigma, isn't he? He's always been a bit secretive and closed off. I think you're good for him, Tara."

"I hope so. But there's something that puzzles me. I don't know if I should bring it up, but you know his house in Newport Beach?"

"Yes, what about it?"

"Well, I've never been there and—"

"Mom! You have to see Mrs. Jensen's garden. It's so beautiful," Jalina ran in, winded. She grabbed Tara's hand and started pulling her to the back door.

"Okay, okay. I'm coming." Tara threw the dish towel on the counter and gave Wendy a helpless look, then followed Jalina outside.

Soon it was nearly nine and they had to leave because Jalina needed to be at rehearsal bright and early the next morning. Tara and Jalina thanked everyone for their hospitality and for including them in their family's Christmas festivities.

Once in the car, Jalina said, "Geoffrey, I really like your family. They're all so nice, but Zak is my favorite."

"What about me?" Geoffrey pouted.

"I mean, besides you, of course, silly. Zak is so cute and sweet. When I'm old enough do you think Wendy will let me babysit sometimes?"

"I'm sure she will," Geoffrey smiled. "I'm glad you like them. Zak told me he likes you, too."

"Really? Yay!"

The next morning, Geoffrey woke up in a frisky mood, glad Christmas was finally over and he wouldn't have to deal with it for another year.

"Let's go for a walk. Come on, get up. Let's go."

"You want to go for a walk *now*?" Tara wiped the sleep out of her eyes.

"Yep. Let's go."

"Okay, sure. I'll get dressed." But when Tara pulled back the covers and sat up, Geoffrey wouldn't let her get out of bed. He pulled her back down and pinned her.

"Geoffrey, what's gotten into you? Do you want to go on a walk or not?"

"Of course I do. Why aren't you up yet?" he teased.

She tried to get up again and he tackled her again. This time he tickled her until she laughed so hard so couldn't breathe. "I've never seen this side of you before. I'm not complaining, but why so playful?"

"Can't I have fun and tease my fiancée if I want to?"

"Fiancée, wow. That's the first time I've heard you say that."

"Having second thoughts?"

"No, of course not. Why would you say that? It just doesn't seem real because we haven't told anyone yet. Since I can't talk about it, I haven't thought that much about it."

"Tara, you know why we can't tell people yet."

"I know. I'm just telling you it doesn't quite feel real to me."

Geoffrey got out of bed.

"Where are you going? I thought we were going to fool

around!"

"I'm not in the mood anymore. Besides, don't you have to take Jalina to rehearsal?"

"Oh crap! I bet she overslept. I gotta go. Thanks, honey."

27

Two Weeks

THE NEXT TWO weeks went downhill fast. It began two days after Christmas when Geoffrey locked himself in his office all day, a pattern he repeated over and over. He claimed he had a headache and said he needed some down time.

At six o'clock Tara poked her head in his office. He was playing a video game on his computer.

"You didn't knock."

"Sorry, I forgot. I just wanted to check in on you and see if you want to join us for dinner. Are you feeling better? How's your headache?"

"Us? Who's 'us?' Is Jalina still here?"

"Yes, I told you earlier we'd have her three weeks in a row. Her dad had to go on another business trip. This is his busiest time of year. He flew to Hong Kong early this morning."

"But this is his week. Can't he get someone else to watch her when it's his week? He's being irresponsible by assuming you'll pick up the slack. He's taking advantage of your kind nature, Tara. You can't let him walk all over you like that."

"Whoa. He is not taking advantage of me. I told him months ago that when he goes out of town, I will take her. I don't care whose week it is or isn't. I don't want someone else watching her—she's *my child* and I love her. I happily take her when Joe can't. I treasure the time I have with her and miss her when she's not here. You don't understand. You're not a parent." Tara stopped to compose herself, relaxing her clenched fists, and taking a deep breath.

"Is that why you've been in here all day? Are you avoiding having to spend time with Jalina?"

"No, of course not. Don't be ridiculous, Tara. I don't feel good. And your shouting at me right now is not helping. I'm not hungry and I don't want dinner. Now, please leave me alone."

"As you wish. And don't worry, you'll have the house to yourself the next four days. Jalina and I have all day rehearsals from nine to four."

"Why do you have to be there?"

"I told you, I signed up to help with props and makeup, remember? And I'm also helping them build and paint the set. There's a lot to do before the show opens."

"Fine. Have fun. Goodbye." He turned around and went back to his game.

Apparently, once Geoffrey finally told Tara the truth about his work situation he'd given up the ruse. He hadn't even bothered to pretend to go into the office at work anymore.

The only time he left the house was to go to the gym. Some nights he even slept in his office. Tara observed that if he'd had a refrigerator and blender in there she'd never see him.

She was glad he told her about his work stress and lack of clients, glad he was being honest with her. But her heart hurt for him and she didn't know how to help him. By telling her the truth, it gave him permission to be moody and stressed out even more. He withdrew so much that Tara wondered if he still loved her.

And worse, she couldn't talk to anybody about it. Geoffrey swore her to secrecy. He didn't want anyone to know, especially his family. He still felt the need to keep up appearances to the outside world.

New Year's Eve Tara took Jalina and Skyler to Skyler's house after rehearsal. She'd arranged a sleepover, hoping to have a nice night with Geoffrey and cheer him up. And to make sure there were no distractions or anything else that might upset him, she took Nala, too. In fact, she'd even taken Nala with her to rehearsals every day. She was a great dog and the kids loved her.

Table set, candles lit, mood music on, Tara got Geoffrey's favorite thin crust 'healthy' pizza and root beer for a night of indulgence. She even slipped into a tight, little black dress. It was a reward she'd bought for herself after losing sixteen pounds in a month.

All her hard work had paid off and she was stronger and had more lean muscle than she'd ever had. She looked and felt better than she had in years. And yet, they hadn't been intimate since Christmas Eve.

Tara went upstairs and softly knocked on the office door, "Geoffrey? May I come in?"

"No." Her hand was already turning the knob when his reply registered. She stopped in her tracks. "I'm just messing with you, Tara. What's up?"

She opened the door and strode in, looking around. She couldn't tell what he'd been doing but had the sensation he was up to something.

"Wow, you look beautiful. What's the occasion?"

"It's New Year's Eve. I thought we'd celebrate with your favorite pizza and have a nice evening downstairs."

"You know I don't care about holidays."

"I know, but maybe you could humor me? It's been a while since we've talked."

"Okay, sure...am I dressed okay?" He had on black sweats and a gray t-shirt.

"Perfect. Everything's ready downstairs. Right this way, sir." Tara smiled, but the smile didn't reach her eyes.

They sat across from each other at the table and ate in silence. Geoffrey didn't comment on the candles or music and kept his eyes downcast.

Finally, he softly asked, "Do you remember what it was like for you when you were depressed?"

Instant tears formed in Tara's eyes. "Yes, I remember," she whispered.

"I have a mild form of depression called dysthymia. In my case, it's a situational depressive disorder caused by financial and job stress. Or, 'lack of job' stress."

"Were you diagnosed, or did you—"

"I diagnosed myself. I'm a trained psychotherapist, Tara. I know the symptoms."

"Okay. How can I help you through this?"

"You can't. All you can do is leave me alone when I ask, give me space, and be patient. I'm sorry. It has nothing to do with you. Please don't take it personally.... I love you, but I'm too stressed right now to have a relationship."

"You don't want a relationship? Are you breaking up with me?"

"No, that came out wrong. I mean, just be patient with

me, okay? I still want to marry you. But if I don't get clients soon, I won't have much of a future to offer you. I'll just be another unemployed bum sponging off his wife."

"Babe, you are not a bum. You'll get clients. It'll happen. I see how hard you work. You're in your office so much I'm jealous of your computer!" Tara laughed.

Geoffrey's blank expression did nothing for her confidence.

"How about we watch a comedy? Laughter is good for the soul, and it'll help take your mind off things, okay?"

"All right. Sorry I'm such a downer."

"It's okay. I get it. Believe me, I've been there. But it'll get better soon, you'll see. Now go sit on the couch and pick out a movie. I'll be right there."

Tara cleared the table and brought their root beers to the living room. She sat down next to Geoffrey and rested her hand in his lap and her head on his shoulder.

"I love you," she whispered.

"Me, too, but can you scoot over a little. I just want to watch the movie."

They watched *The Hangover*. As the movie progressed, Geoffrey laughed a few times and seemed to relax a bit. But Tara also noticed his demeanor toward her seemed to change.

He took the remote control and pretended to stab her with it. Then, he lightly punched her in the stomach a few times.

Tara wanted to cheer him up but since she hadn't grown up with brothers she wasn't used to play fighting. She awkwardly jabbed him in the ribs and tried to laugh it off.

"Wouldn't it be weird if I killed you in the middle of the night?"

"What? That's not funny! Don't say things like that. I

don't like that kind of teasing."

"I'm just joking, geez. Relax. You're so sensitive."

The next morning, while getting ready to go to the gym, Geoffrey waved a flash drive in Tara's face and made swooshing noises pretending it was a knife slicing her cheeks. She came unhinged. "Don't you ever threaten me."

"What are you talking about? I'm not threatening you. I'm just messing around."

"Well, I don't like that kind of messing around. It feels like you want to hit me and I won't tolerate being hit."

"Oh, you won't *tolerate* it?" He raised his hand and Tara flinched. "Shit, Tara. I'm hurt. I can't believe you think I'd actually hit you…that you think I'm a batterer."

Tara stood still, unsure of what to say next. She met his eyes and saw something cold and almost evil in them. She looked down at the floor and tried to speak. "I know you wouldn't hurt me. I just don't like that kind of kidding.

He grabbed her arm and stared into her eyes.

"Ouch! You're hurting me. Stop it. Geoffrey, what are you doing?"

Geoffrey released his grip and Tara could see a red fingerprint imprint on her bicep. She wondered if it would bruise.

"Drive yourself to the gym." He left. They took two separate cars to the gym and ignored each other there, not talking to each other the rest of the day.

Tara drove to Skyler's and talked with Nicolee for a while before coming home. She needed to cool off. The girls told her about their fun night and everyone wished each other a 'Happy New Year' before Tara brought Jalina and Nala home.

Geoffrey didn't come to bed until three in the morning and left again at six. He slept in his shorts, on top of the bed, with only a thin blanket as a cover. He stayed on the edge of the king-sized bed, widening the distance between them as much as possible. When he got up, he re-made his side of the bed, left quietly, and locked himself in his office.

Tara got up at seven, made her shake, checked her email, and wondered when she was going to kick him out. *But I can't kick him out when he's down. Where will he go? I couldn't live with myself if I did that.*

She was losing her patience. She wanted to be understanding and loving but enough was enough. She had a big heart and forgave many things but even Tara had boundaries.

Geoffrey came downstairs and walked to the kitchen. Tara ignored him. As if he could read her mind, he did something unexpected—he held her.

He pulled her up off a chair at the dining table where she'd been working on her laptop, pulled her close to him and wrapped his arms around her. She stiffened at first but then her body slowly relaxed as she gave in, soon dissolving into tears as she cried in his arms. It felt good to be held by him.

"Everything's going to be okay," he soothed. "You're making this more than it is." He calmed her down. He made her feel better.

28

Lies

SCHOOL WAS BACK in session and opening week of Jalina's play had arrived. The show opened Thursday and Joe would be back in time to see closing night, Saturday. As opening night grew closer, Jalina got more excited.

Tara needed help with the stage makeup and called Miranda, a professional makeup artist she worked with on *The Bad Wife*.

"Hey, Miranda, do you want to help me with makeup for a kid's theater production?"

"What's the show?"

"Beauty and the Beast."

"I love that show. And the Beast will be so much fun to create. I'd love to, Tara."

"Great, thank you so much. The Beast's makeup is a bit too challenging for me and we don't have the budget for an elaborate costume."

"I have a ton of ideas. Don't worry about a thing. Consider the Beast mine."

"Thank you, Miranda. This will mean so much to the kids. Our first rehearsal with makeup is tomorrow at 3:30 p.m."

"I'll be there."

"Awesome. See you tomorrow."

Tara hung up and contemplated going to the gym. It was nine in the morning and she'd already taken Nala for a walk, Jalina to school, and recruited Miranda. Just then Geoffrey came downstairs, dressed in workout clothes.

"I'm going to the gym," he announced, and walked out to the garage before Tara could respond.

It's now or never. Be calm. Deep breaths. I can do this.

Tara went upstairs to Geoffrey's office. Fortunately, the door didn't have a lock on it. *If it did, he'd probably keep it locked all the time.* He was in there so much lately and had been guarded and secretive the few times she disturbed him. He'd been very quick to switch his screen to black or the screensaver. She had to see what had been holding his attention for hours on end.

Luckily, his computer had only been in sleep mode and she was able to get on the Internet without a password. She quickly checked his browser history but it only showed her the last two sites he'd been on. *He must be deleting his search history daily. Okay, Mister, what are you hiding?* She clicked the first link and was directed to the home page of an Internet dating site, Match.com.

An image of his smiling face stared at her, complete with a dating profile. Tara's heart sank. He'd sent 30 emails and 65 winks, and had been active on the site five minutes ago. *Five minutes ago!*

She opened an email he'd sent to Bambi-xox. He'd given her his phone number and encouraged her to call him.

What the? She opened and read all the sent emails.

The color drained from her face and her heart thudded in her ears. *Who is this man living in my house? Why did he propose to me if he's busy flirting with all these other women? Why all the lies?*

"What's going on?" she shouted.

Nala nosed the door open, sat down next to Tara and put her head in Tara's lap.

"You knew all along, didn't you, girl?" She stroked the soft fur and rubbed the spot behind her ears. "I should have paid more attention. You didn't like him at first sniff. Oh, Nala, what am I going to do?"

Nala's tail thumped against the floor in reply as her soft brown eyes held Tara's gaze.

"What am I missing? What else is he hiding from me?"

The hum of the garage door opening reverberated through the floorboards.

"Oh crap, he's here. Hurry, Nala, we have to get out of here before he comes in." Tara quickly put everything back how she found. She called Nala and they left Geoffrey's office and closed the door.

"Tara? I'm hooome," Geoffrey called out.

She ran downstairs and greeted him with a big smile. But she couldn't go through with the phony act. She was a horrible liar.

While he was still standing in the hall by the garage door, Geoffrey froze.

"Tara? What's wrong? You look upset about something. Are you okay?"

She was shaking as she spit out the words, "What are you doing on Match?"

"What the hell are you doing in my office? On my computer? That's an invasion of privacy."

"But it's in *my* home! You're not going to turn this one

around on me. Answer the question. Why are you on Match?"

"Relax, Tara, it's harmless. I'm hurt that you don't trust me. What do we have if we don't have trust?"

"Seriously? I caught you on a *dating site* and you're the hurt one?"

"Tara, I'm not cheating on you." He walked to her and she backed away. "I'm just talking to people. I'm trying to get clients for my practice."

"On a dating site? By flirting with them? Are you kidding me? Am I not enough for you? I thought you loved me. I thought we had something rare and special. I was in love with you—planning to spend my life with you.

"That's why I've stood by you through this temporary time of unfortunate circumstances. That's why I've tried to be patient and supportive and loving—for you. Apparently, I'm still gullible, naive, and clueless."

Geoffrey wouldn't look at her. He sat down at the dining table and took off his shoes. Before he could think of a way to manipulate her or talk his way out of it, she blurted out, "I can't do this anymore."

Without any trace of emotion, he simply said, "Okay."

"Do you even care?"

"I care, but I'm stressed. We've talked about this. I'll go stay with my parents until my house sells. I don't want to talk about this right now. I'm not feeling well today."

"You never want to talk about stuff. What a messed up, dysfunctional relationship we have."

"You don't know what you're talking about. Don't throw labels around you don't understand."

"You don't think I know what dysfunctional means? Just because it's one of your psychobabble terms I'm not allowed to use the word?"

"You're upset. I'm not going to talk to you right now,"

Geoffrey stood and walked up the stairs.

"Of course I'm upset. Where are you going?"

"I told you. I don't feel well. I'm going to lie down in my easy chair in my office. We'll talk about this later." He looked defeated and sad…so very, very sad.

What have I done? Did we just break up? Am I that cold-hearted? How will I tell Jalina?

Geoffrey didn't come to bed that night. He spent the night in his office and Tara tossed and turned. She wanted to comfort him, wanted to tell him she'd made a mistake and would take him back. *But I deserve to be treated better than this.* She went back and forth all night. *Do I really have the nerve to kick him out? To force him to stay with his parents?*

He hadn't said a word about his house or his realtor. As far as Tara knew, the repairs from the flood should be done by now. The house had been on the market for a month and Tara hadn't heard about any offers. She didn't understand why he couldn't just go back to living in his house until he got a buyer. She didn't understand a lot of things.

29

Detective Reynolds

AFTER SCHOOL THE next day the kids had their first rehearsal with makeup. It was also the technical rehearsal where they tested the lights and sound, and used microphones for the first time as well. There were a few areas that needed smoothing out. But as the saying goes, "Bad dress rehearsal, good opening night." The cast and crew were optimistic.

Wednesday morning, Tara got a call from a number she didn't recognize so she let it go to voicemail. When she checked the message a few minutes later, a tight knot formed in her stomach. The message was from a Detective Dave Reynolds and he was calling about a Jeff Jensen. Even though she knew him as Geoffrey, she knew they were the same person. She remembered his family calling him Jeff, and quickly correcting themselves, at Thanksgiving. The Detective said the matter was urgent so she took a deep breath and called him back, brows furrowed, unaware she was holding her breath.

"Detective Reynolds," he answered on the first ring.

"Hello, Detective. This is Tara Spencer. I received a message to call you."

"Yes. Hello, Tara. Thank you for returning my call," the detective paused. "I'm afraid I have to deliver some unpleasant news about Jeff Jensen. I have reason to believe you may be in danger."

"Do you mean Dr. Jensen? And he told me his name is Geoffrey. Are you sure you have the right person?"

"Half-Japanese, five foot ten, physically fit, with a tattoo of a samurai sword on his right shoulder?"

"Yes, that's Geoffrey."

"Look, I don't know what cockamamie story he's told you or what made up name he goes by these days but he's no doctor. Are you alone now?"

He's a fraud? Dazed by what she'd just learned Tara replied, "He's in his office."

"The one he shares with Dr. Nguyen? We've had eyes on that. He hasn't been there in weeks."

"No, here. He hasn't had any clients lately. He stays here in his home office most days." Realizing Geoffrey could possibly overhear her conversation, Tara stepped outside.

"I see. How long has he lived with you, Ms. Spencer?"

"A little over a month. He moved in December 3. Why? What's this all about? You said I might be in danger?"

"I've been tracking Jeff, er, Geoffrey Jensen for several years. Ever since his first wife, Gigi Jensen, was reported missing fifteen years ago."

"Missing? He told me she was a model in Europe."

"She never made it that far. Missing fourteen years until we got a break in the case last year. We found her washed up on the shore of Catalina Island. Well, what was left of her anyway. Got a positive id on the dental records. Such a tragedy, too. A gorgeous 22-year-old supermodel," Detective Reynolds cleared his throat. "We think she was murdered."

"Murdered?" Tara blanched and covered her mouth with her hand.

"Ma'am, we have reason to believe Jeff…or Geoffrey, whatever, may have killed his first wife. We have records of domestic calls and probable abuse with his second wife and we fear you may be next. I wanted to bring him in two years ago on a domestic call his stepson reported but I hadn't made detective yet and I was outranked. I didn't have anything I could make stick."

"And now? Can you prove he killed his ex-wife?"

"Not yet, but I'm close. I'm warning you before he figures out we're onto him, 'specially since we're digging around in his past. If he gets wind of it, there's no telling what he'll do. Desperate men do desperate things and I want to make sure you're okay before I pull the trigger on this."

"Do you think he would hurt me?"

"I don't know, but I'd be careful if I were you. Have you noticed any suspicious behavior?"

"Yes, he holes up in his office all day and doesn't go to work at all anymore. Lately, he even spends the night in there. He only leaves to go to the gym. He never misses a workout."

"Are you sure he's going to the gym? What gym?"

"No, I'm not sure. He belongs to two gyms. 24 Hour Fitness and Fitness One. He always leaves in gym clothes but I guess he could be going somewhere else. We used to work out together but he hasn't wanted to go with me lately. He might be going to his house, I suppose."

"His house?"

"Yes, he has a house in Newport Beach. He's been trying to sell it, but it got flooded, so he moved in with me while they fix it."

"Have you ever seen this house?"

"No, why?"

"He hasn't owned a home in Newport Beach for two years. He sold it when he left his second wife."

"He what? Could I have the address please?"

"Sure. I'll give you the addresses of his last two residences. Go ahead and check 'em out. When you're convinced I'm on your side, call me back. This is my private cell. Call any time."

Tara hurried back inside, found a pen and pad of paper, and wrote down the addresses of his house in Newport Beach and his apartment in Costa Mesa. Her hands shook as she wrote.

As soon as she hung up with the detective, Tara jumped in her car and drove to Newport Beach. It was nearly ten and morning traffic had cleared. She drove to the address the detective had given her hoping to see an empty house with a For Sale sign out front but, deep down, she knew she wouldn't.

The house was every bit as impressive and grand as Geoffrey said it was but the black Mercedes in the driveway and floral welcome mat with "The Roberts Family" emblazoned on it…let her know that it wasn't empty, Geoffrey didn't own it and he'd lied to her. *Again.*

Tara raced off to the next address, with a sinking feeling in the pit of her stomach.

When she arrived at the apartment on the second story of the apartment complex, she knocked on the door next to Geoffrey's old apartment. If what the detective said was true, he'd only moved out a month ago. Chances were good his neighbors had at least seen him.

The door creaked open a crack to reveal a young woman in her twenties, peering at Tara with big eyes.

"Hello, sorry to bother you. I promise I'm not selling anything," Tara tried to laugh. "I just want to ask you about the man who used to live next door to you. Did you know him?"

"Oh! Yeah, he was a real nut job." She enthusiastically swung open the door, eager to dish about her former neighbor. "The day he moved out he was acting all crazy. He threw furniture and a bunch of stuff away in the dumpster. And I saw him single-handedly take a mattress and box spring and hurl them over the railing, right there behind you," she pointed.

"Before he left, he went downstairs and threw those in the dumpster, too. They were perfectly good and practically brand new. My husband and I dragged them out of there and are using the bed for our daughter. Is that okay? We're not in trouble or anything, are we?"

"No, of course not. I'm sure if something's in the dumpster it's fair game. One man's trash is another's treasure, right? Thank you for your time."

"Sure, no problem. Is he in some kinda trouble? Are you a cop?"

"No, just a concerned citizen. Have a nice day."

Tara walked back to her car and drove home. *What kind of sick game is he playing? He sold his house two years ago, moved into an apartment, and threw away furniture and his bed before moving in with me? My head hurts. Was the detective right? Is Geoffrey some kind of psychopath? I have to get him out of my house!*

Suddenly she remembered Mr. Crenshaw and how he'd freaked out when he ran into her at Target. She thought his behavior was odd, but now she had a feeling there was more to it. And she had to find out.

When Tara got home she found the volunteer roster from Jalina's class and dialed the number for Bart Crenshaw. She went outside on the pretense of taking Nala for a walk in case Geoffrey was paying attention to what she was doing. Mr. Crenshaw answered on the second ring, "Hello?"

"Hi, Mr. Crenshaw?"

"Yes. Who is this?"

"This is Tara Spencer. I'm calling you because—"

"I have nothing to say to you."

"Wait! Please, don't hang up. Please, I beg you. I think I might be in danger and I need to ask you a question."

"What?" he hesitated. "What do you want to know?"

"Remember that day I saw you at Target?"

"Yes."

"Why did you run away? Did something happen between you and Geoffrey?"

"What makes you say that?"

"He has recently revealed to me that he has some violent tendencies."

"You can say that again."

"Did something happen at the laser tag place that day? Did he threaten you somehow?"

"I'll say! He damn near broke a rib, if you call that a threat." He spit out the words.

"He did what?"

"He told me to stay away from you and Jalina and never speak to you again. He made it sound like if I did he would kill me. Then he punched and kicked me in the ribs and back until I nearly passed out. I believed him. When I saw you in Target that day, I panicked. I've got a family to think about. I don't need this crap. Look, lady, I wish you well, but I can't be involved. If I were you I'd get as far away from him as I could—now."

"I am so sorry that happened to you. I had no idea. Thank you for telling me. I won't bother you again and, you can rest assured, I won't tell anyone about this. Right now, I need to consider my own safety. Thank you for your time."

"Goodbye." He hung up before Tara could say anything else.

What is happening? Geoffrey beat up Mr. Crenshaw? But why? Tara had no idea what to do with any of this. She felt sick to her stomach. The bile rose up in the back of her throat as she swallowed it back down.

30

Beauty and the Beast

JALINA'S OPENING NIGHT for *Beauty and the Beast* was mere hours away. Tara was in the bathroom at the theater and had a killer headache. She held a paper towel over her eyes to block out the light while she tried to process all she'd learned this week—especially in the last twenty-four hours.

Trying to piece it all together she wondered how to get Geoffrey to leave without putting herself in danger. They hadn't spoken to each other since Monday, three days ago.

He'd come in her bedroom in the middle of the night last night but she pretended to be asleep. He lay down next to her but was gone when she woke up this morning. She didn't even know how she'd managed to fall asleep at all, considering her fiancée might be a deranged killer. She felt like she'd just stared at the ceiling all night willing morning to come. She was numb and sleep-deprived. She wondered how she was even functioning.

Thankfully, it had been easy to avoid him. He stayed in his office and she'd spent more time at the theater. She kept busy helping the other volunteer parents fold programs and get everything set up for tonight.

An hour before curtain, Geoffrey sent her a text. "Hey, are you coming home before the show? Where's my ticket?"

"I'll put it at will call for you. I'll meet you at our seats right before the show."

"Okay. See you then. I'm looking forward to it. Tell Jalina I wish her good luck. -xo"

"Will do, thanks."

Rattled, Tara stared at his messages not comprehending why he still wanted to see the show.

Miranda did an excellent job on the Beast's makeup and mask. Everyone was in awe. Belle looked radiant and Tara was honored to be able to do her daughter's makeup. Jalina/Belle looked like a mini-version of the Disney animated Belle, with her big brown eyes and long brown hair. She was positively in her element.

"You look wonderful, sweetheart!" Tara gushed. "Are you nervous?"

"Yeah, I'm super nervous, but I'm also super excited. Belle has always been my favorite princess. I just hope I don't mess up."

"You won't. You got this! I know it. You've worked so hard for this role. Now it's time to get out there and shine like the star you are. Relax and enjoy it. You know this part forward and backward. Just do your best, have fun, and everything will fall into place. Have a great show. I love you."

Tara knew better than to use the showbiz term, 'break a leg.' Ever since Jalina actually did break her leg, she'd hated the saying. It had happened at a play rehearsal over a year ago.

While on a break, the kids hung out in the courtyard so the director could have a parent meeting. Jalina was walking with Skyler. As they rounded a corner, another kid from the play flew toward her while riding a bike. But the corner and a giant bush blocked his view.

He hadn't seen Jalina or Skyler until it was too late. His bike ploughed into her, hitting her left leg and breaking both bones in her shin. The surgeon had called it a combined transverse tibia-fibula fracture.

Every kid in their theater group witnessed the accident that day. Some of them were traumatized. Most of them just couldn't stop talking about it. For a while, Jalina was known as 'broken leg girl.'

"Thanks, Mommy."

Tara gave her daughter a light squeeze, careful not to ruffle her costume or smudge her makeup. "I'll be right out there, baby." She blew her a kiss and went down the stairs to find her seat in the auditorium.

Dorey, sitting in the second row, waved at her, "Hey, Lady. Are you as nervous as Jalina is for her big Broadway debut?"

"Dorey! It's so good to see you. I have so much to tell you…but, I can't right now."

"Tara? What's wrong? You look like you've seen a ghost. Are you okay?"

"Not really, no. You were right."

"Naturally," she grinned. "About what?"

"About everything. I'm engaged to a monster."

"What? You're engaged? Fuck. Shit. Damn. Hell. What did that SOB do to you?"

"Shhh, keep your voice down. You're surrounded by children, remember?"

"Sorry. What's going on?"

"There's no time. I'll have to tell you later. I better get to my seat before he sees us."

Dorey grabbed Tara's hand and squeezed it. "Be careful."

"Always."

Nicolee McKeever and her husband, Phil, waved at Tara from their seats in the fourth row. "This is it! It's the girls' big night. Do you think they're ready?" Nicolee asked.

"They're ready," Tara smiled. "And your Mrs. Potts is fabulous! I got to watch the dress rehearsal last night and your daughter is very talented."

"Thank you!" she beamed with pride.

Tara took her seat in the middle of the fifth row. Geoffrey was already seated in his, reading his program. "Well, hello, stranger. Did you get everything done in time? This play isn't going to be a dud, is it?"

"Hi, Geoffrey," Tara smiled tersely. "Yes, everything's right on track. The kids have worked very hard. It should be a good show. But remember, they are kids. This isn't Broadway so don't expect too much, okay?"

"No kidding, I'm not an idiot."

"I know. I just don't want you to have unrealistic expectations."

"Don't worry. If Jalina sucks, I promise I won't tell her to her face." Tara winced, but let it go.

Geoffrey reached for Tara's hand and she forced herself not to recoil from his touch or pull away. Just then, the lights went down and the music started, much to her relief.

Jalina and the cast of *Beauty and the Beast* received a standing ovation and she was given a beautiful bouquet of red roses. Opening night was a raving success. Tara was so proud of her talented daughter she thought her heart would burst. At least the performance helped take her

mind off her current problems and how to handle
Geoffrey. She was afraid to rile him, not knowing what he
was capable of doing.

After the show, Jalina wanted to go to Denny's with her
cast mates, an opening night tradition. Tara volunteered to
drive a car full of girls over and breathed a sigh of relief
when Geoffrey said he didn't want to go. Since they'd
taken two separate cars to the play, Geoffrey drove himself
home and Tara and the girls went to Denny's.

Everyone congratulated Jalina on a great show. She
humbly deflected and told each person how great they
were, but inside, she nearly burst with glee. She was
oblivious to her mom's anxious mood. Tara tried to keep
up a brave front, smiling and chatting with the other
moms, while thirty kids sugared up at Denny's.

When they got home, after eleven on a school night,
Tara hugged Jalina tight, congratulated her for the tenth
time on her stellar performance, and sent her upstairs to
brush her teeth and go to bed. After taking Nala on a
quick walk she locked up and steeled herself to go upstairs.
She let Nala into Jalina's room finding her daughter already
slumbering.

With her hand hesitating on the door knob of her own
room she took a deep breath and eased the door open.
The room was dark and Geoffrey wasn't there. The tension
drained out of her face and shoulders as she realized he
probably fell asleep in his office.

Just to be sure, she tiptoed to his office and cracked the
door open just enough to see him sacked out in his easy
chair. *Thank you, God.* She sent up a silent prayer, closed the
door, and went to bed.

She slept fitfully as her mind raced through all the things
she'd discovered about her darling Geoffrey the past few
days.

Why did he lie to me? What was he hiding? Did he kill his first wife? Was he a killer?

Chills ran through her as she realized how close she had come to *marrying* him. *What was I thinking?*

31

The Jig is Up

ONE DOWN, THREE more to go.

Jalina's play ran two more nights, with a Saturday matinée. Tara focused on helping with the play and staying at the theater as much as possible, avoiding Geoffrey at all costs. She even kept Nala with her as much as she could. The kids adored Nala and she became their unofficial mascot. *There's no way I'm leaving my dog alone with that psycho.* The thought chilled her.

It was finally closing night. Joe was back in town and promised not to miss his daughter's first leading role. True to his word, he sent Tara a text that afternoon.

"I'm back. What time does Jalina's show start?"

"Welcome back. Starts at 7:00 pm. She'll be thrilled you can make it. I'll leave a ticket for you at will call."

"Perfect. Thanks."

A few minutes later, she got a text from Geoffrey. *Great,*

what does he want? She opened the message to reveal he wanted a closing night ticket. *What?* She didn't understand why he wanted to see it again when she distinctly remembered their conversation a week earlier.

"How many times do you want to see Jalina's show?" Tara had asked.

"You're kidding, right? I only need to see it once, thanks. Why? How many times are you going to see it?"

"I watch all of her performances."

"*All* of them? Why on earth would you do that? You seriously watch every performance?"

"Yes."

"That's crazy. I don't get why anybody would want to see a show more than once… would want to sit through a two-hour ordeal…"

"Okay, let me put it this way. If Jalina played basketball would you watch one game of the season and figure if you've seen one game you've seen them all?"

"Of course not. That's ridiculous. Every game is different."

"That's how it is with live theater, too. It might be the same lines but no two shows are exactly alike. Just as you wouldn't dream of missing a game I'm not going to miss a single show—especially when my daughter has the lead part and this is important to her."

"Fair enough," Geoffrey had said, dismissing the conversation.

Tara bristled at the memory and sighed. Now she looked down at the blinking cursor on her phone and texted back, "I'll leave a ticket for you at will call and meet you at our seats like last time."

Joe spotted Geoffrey in the lobby. He strode over to him and shook his hand, "Hey, Geoffrey. I'm so glad I ran into you."

"Oh? Why is that?"

"I want to thank you for taking such good care of Tara. She's been through a lot and deserves a nice guy like you. I couldn't be happier for the two of you. It also means a lot to me that you're here tonight and supportive of my daughter. Jalina looks up to you and I know it means a lot to her, too."

"What are you talking about?"

"Your engagement. Tara told me."

"She what? When?"

"Christmas morning when she picked up Jalina. She was bursting with joy."

"Was she? Well, Joe, that's a problem for me. You see, I asked her not to tell anybody yet. We're not announcing it or making it official until I…I mean, it's just not set yet."

"I see."

"No, Joe, I don't think you do. But let me spell it out for you. I'm not comfortable with Tara and you talking all the time. She's not your wife anymore. Your marriage is over. Leave her alone."

"We're raising a child together. Whether you like it or not that means we need to talk to each other once in a while. Besides, we're friends."

"That's what I mean. I don't want you to be friends. You can be co-parents without the friendliness. Just leave her alone—got it?"

"If I didn't know better I'd think that was a threat."

"Listen, buddy, you can take it however you want. I just want you to stay the hell out of Tara's business."

"And if I don't?"

"I'll make it so you regret it."

"Oh, so you're a tough guy, huh?"

"You don't want to mess with me. Stay away from us."

The lights in the lobby flashed, the final warning that it was time to take their seats.

Joe and Geoffrey glared at each other one last time then each went to their respective seats. Tara knew better than to have them sit close to each other. She was already seated when Geoffrey got there. He seemed agitated and his breathing was unsteady. "Is everything okay?" she whispered.

"Everything's fine, just fine." He said with gritted teeth staring at the stage. She knew better than to keep prodding so she dropped it.

During intermission Geoffrey left Tara's side to use the restroom. Joe jogged over, the color drained from his face.

"Tara, we need to talk."

"Joe? What's wrong?"

"Your fiancée is a psycho and he threatened me."

"He what?"

"He told me to leave you alone. He said he doesn't want us being friends anymore and that I'm to stay the hell out of your life. He's trying to freeze me out. Does he want to take over completely? Does he want to be Jalina's dad and replace me? Because I will never allow that to happen."

"Joe, it's okay. Calm down. I'm ending it. It's over."

"What? The engagement?"

"Yes, all of it. As soon as Jalina's play is over I'm going to ask him to move out. Tonight. A lot happened while you were gone but I'll have to tell you later. You better go back to your seat before he gets back."

"Tara, you're shaking. What's going on?"

"There's no time to explain; go back to your seat before he sees you."

"Tara—"

"Joe, I'm serious. For once, don't argue with me. You're not safe. Just go! I'll fill you in later."

"But Tara—" Her wild, frantic eyes cut him off this time. He'd never seen her like that, the look of fear and panic in her eyes unnerved him. He shut his mouth, got up, and moved to his own seat a few rows back.

Just then Geoffrey strode down the aisle toward Tara. Joe didn't take his eyes off them.

After the final curtain went down Tara told Geoffrey she'd see him at home as soon as she dropped the girls off at the cast party. She got up to leave and he grabbed her arm.

"I want to congratulate the star," he demanded.

She managed a smile and said, "Sorry, there's no time. I have to help backstage and then the cast party starts right away. You can congratulate her tomorrow, okay?"

Geoffrey said nothing but continued holding Tara's arm his grip tightening. His eyes stared blankly somewhere beyond her, searching.

"Let go of me," Tara snapped. "Geoffrey, you're hurting me."

He woke out of his reverie and released his grip. Finally, he nodded and smiled too big, teeth clenched. "You're right, now's not the time. I'll have plenty of time with her tomorrow. Go have fun."

Over my dead body, Tara thought on her way backstage. She didn't want Geoffrey anywhere near Jalina. If she was lucky he'd move out tomorrow while Jalina was still at Skyler's and they'd never see him again.

An hour later, after dropping off the girls and making arrangements with Nicolee for Jalina to spend the night after the cast party, Tara drove home. Her knuckles were white as she gripped the steering wheel. Fueled with rage and adrenaline at his threats to Joe, Tara stomped in ready to do battle with Geoffrey. She found him in the living room, watching *Prom Night*, a 1980 slasher movie.

She sat down in the chair next to the couch and studied him. He didn't acknowledge her. She cleared her throat and said, "Geoffrey, we need to talk."

"I'm watching a movie."

Exasperated, she sighed and launched into it anyway. "You had no right to threaten Joe tonight. He told me everything."

"Of course he did."

"I want you out. It's over."

"Okay."

"So you'll move out tomorrow?"

"Sure. Now let me watch this movie in peace—please."

That was easy…too easy. Tara walked away unsteadily, her knees wobbly and her body still amped up for the argument that didn't happen; nervous energy coursing through her veins. She took Nala upstairs with her and barely slept, wondering if Geoffrey would actually move out without a fight.

32

Jalina

THE NEXT MORNING Tara woke up with Nala on the bed next to her. Geoffrey had fallen asleep on the couch with the TV on. A loud crash woke up Tara at two in the morning. Disoriented, she went downstairs to find a sleeping Geoffrey. Some horror flick was on and Tara figured out the crash sound that woke her had come from the blaring television. She turned off the TV and went back to bed.

Now 7:30, she threw on some sweats to take Nala outside. "Come on, girl. Let's go for a quick walk."

When they got downstairs the couch was empty. Tara looked in the garage and Geoffrey's car was gone. She figured he probably went to the gym. Somehow with everything going on he never seemed to miss a workout.

Or maybe he'd gone to his parents' house to tell his mom about their break up and make arrangements to stay with them. Hopefully, that was the case. With any luck he'd have a storage unit rented, a moving truck booked, and be out of here in the next couple days.

Except it was still early Sunday morning. Tara knew Geoffrey's mom liked to sleep in on weekends. *So where is he?* She shook it off and tried not to think about it as she took Nala outside.

Tara decided to skip her workout and hopped in the shower. When Geoffrey still hadn't returned by 9:30, she left the house to pick up Jalina from Skyler's. She was eager to see her daughter and wanted to hear about the cast party and how much fun they'd had.

As Tara pulled up to the quiet house, her stomach suddenly felt queasy and her hands were cold and clammy. She shook it off and knocked on the door.

Nicolee answered the door. "Hey, Tara. What's up? Did Jalina forget something?"

"What? No. I mean, I'm here to pick her up," panic rising in her voice as she realized Jalina wasn't there.

"Really? That's odd. Geoffrey already got her a while ago. He said you wanted him to get her so you could cook up a big breakfast of her favorite foods and surprise her when she got home. He said it was to celebrate how good she was in the play…"

Nicolee's voice trailed off and she stopped talking when she saw the color drain from Tara's face. "Tara? What's wrong? Was Geoffrey not supposed to pick her up?"

Tears sprang to Tara's eyes as the reality of the situation hit her. "No, he wasn't. When did you say he got her?"

"Um…"

"Nicolee, I need to know. What time was it? Did he say where he was taking her?"

"Yeah, uh, it was eight o'clock. The girls were still sleeping and I had to wake them up. I told him she hadn't eaten yet and he said you were making a big breakfast at home for her. He said he was bringing her home—to you. I don't understand why you're here..."

"They didn't come home."

"What?"

"I broke up with him last night. I told him I wanted him gone today. Nicolee, I kicked him out."

"Oh my—"

"Geoffrey has Jalina! He kidnapped Jalina! I have to call Joe!"

"Oh my gosh! That's terrible! I am so sorry...what can I do to help?"

Nicolee hugged Tara, but she was already too numb to feel it and didn't want the sympathy. She pulled away and choked out, "Pray."

She ran back to her car, grabbed her purse and dug through it. She gasped, "I left my phone at home! I've got to get home. In case she's there or he calls. Call Joe!"

"I'll call the police too."

"No! Don't. There's a detective I can call. Geoffrey is un-hinged. Just call Joe and tell him to meet me at my place." Tara drove off before Nicolee could answer.

When Tara got home she found her phone sitting on the dining table. There were four missed calls. And they were all from Geoffrey. *No voicemails. No! He didn't leave a message. Now what?*

The phone rang in her hand and she jumped. It was Joe.

"Tara, what's going on? Nicolee called me and said that Geoffrey took Jalina. Where did he take her?"

"I don't know. He called but I'd left my phone at home. I just got here. Where are you?"

"I'm on my way. I'll be there in five minutes. Don't call him until I get there," he hung up.

Pacing and staring at her phone Tara tried to calm down

and think where Geoffrey might take Jalina. She ran up to his office to see if he'd left any clues. She turned on his computer but the login screen came up. "No!"

Joe burst through the front door. "Have you heard anything?"

"I'm up here," she called out.

Joe ran up the stairs to find Tara sitting at a computer. "What are you doing?"

"I'm trying to login to Geoffrey's computer to see if I can find any clues but I don't know his password. Nothing I've tried works."

"We don't have time for that. He could call any minute. Have you tried calling Jalina?"

"Not yet."

"Why would he take her?" Joe asked as he called Jalina's cell phone.

"To get back at me? I broke up with him last night. I don't think he'll hurt her. He's just punishing me for breaking up with him."

"You don't *think* he'll hurt her? What is that supposed to mean?"

A phone rang in the house.

Joe and Tara both ran into Jalina's room to discover her little LG Neon white and green slider phone sitting on her nightstand. She was always forgetting to take her phone with her, a constant thorn in Tara's side. It was her first cell phone and still fairly new. She wasn't accustomed to relying on it yet. Until now, she hadn't even needed it.

A sharp pang seared through Tara's insides as the reality of their situation hit her.

"So…where the fuck did he take my daughter?" Joe demanded.

"I don't know! Can't you see I'm trying to figure that out?" Tears stung her eyes and her breaths grew shallow.

"No you don't. You don't get to fall apart on me, do you hear me? You've gotta keep it together, Tara. Our daughter needs you…. Think. Where would he take her?"

Tara closed her eyes and took three deep breaths, inhaling, holding it, and exhaling slowly just like Geoffrey taught her. *Be mindful. Get a grip.*

She willed herself to calm down picturing a serene lake, placid and beautiful. Her racing heart slowed a bit and her ears stopped ringing. *This really works.* She opened her eyes and looked around. They were still standing in Jalina's room.

Her phone rang in her still trembling hand. She looked at it. "It's him."

"Answer it!" Joe shouted.

"Hello? Geoffrey? Where are you?"

"I told you last night. I want to spend time with Jalina today. I'm ensuring we get lots of quality time together."

"That sounds nice. Where are you taking her?"

"I can't tell you that. It will spoil the surprise. Why didn't you answer the first four times I called?"

"I left my phone home when I went to pick up Jalina from Skyler's. Geoffrey, what surprise are you talking about?"

"You'll see."

"May I please talk to her?"

"Sure, since you asked so nice. But don't try anything funny. I'll know." He took the phone away from his ear and passed it to Jalina, "Hey, Jalina. Your mom wants to talk to you."

"Hi Mommy. We're going on an adventure." Tara was relieved to hear Jalina's cheerful voice.

"Jalina! Where are you, baby? Are you okay?"

"I'm fine," Jalina seemed confused. "Mommy, are you crying? Geoffrey said he's taking me somewhere really cool but that it's a surprise. It's okay. It'll be fun; he promised."

"Are you in his car? Do you know where you are?"

"Yeah, his car is so cool. It goes super fast. It's a sports car."

"Yeah, honey, it's pretty cool. But do you know where you are?"

"Um, we're on a freeway."

"The one going to Los Angeles or the one going to—"

"Nice try. I told you not to try to find out where we are. You'll know when I'm ready for you to know. We'll be in touch. And Tara?"

She swallowed hard, "Yes?"

"Keep your phone with you from now on."

"Geoffrey, wait!" Tara stared at the blank phone as if waiting for it to come back to life then set it down. "He hung up."

"What's going on? Where's he taking her?" Joe asked.

"He won't tell me. He said it's a surprise. But he let me talk to her and she sounds happy, so that's good. She's not scared and doesn't suspect anything so at least he's still being nice to her. That's a good sign, right?"

33

Geoffrey

GEOFFREY WOKE UP at six o'clock that Sunday morning back stiff from sleeping on the couch. He didn't want to wake Tara so he packed a few odds and ends in a duffle bag and planned to shower at the gym. He went in his office and carefully took his katana off the wall then placed it in the bag. *Good. It fits.* He zipped up the bag and headed to the gym.

His workout this morning was therapeutic as he went over his plans for the day. He visualized each step while deadlifting 350 pounds. Methodically, he went over the steps again, memorizing them. This wasn't a rehearsal. He had to get it right.

After his workout the invigorating cold shower woke up all his senses. He felt alive and ready to take on the world, or at least Tara's kid.

Did Tara think she could get rid of me that easily? That stupid bitch. She needs be taught a lesson and what better way to teach her than with her own daughter. Since dealing with my nightmare of a stepson, Brayden, I've learned how to get kids to like me. It's simple; just pretend to like the shit they're into. Ever since that day at the laser tag place, I'm Jalina's hero. I've got that kid wrapped around my finger.

Picking up Jalina at Skyler's house was like taking candy from a baby. He found the house easy enough, too. He'd been there with Tara a couple times when she'd picked her up or dropped her off and the mom was a push-over. *She'd believe whatever garbage spilled out of my mouth.*

He didn't mean to get there so early but he had to beat Tara there and he wasn't sure what time she'd planned on picking the kid up. The plan would fail if Tara saw him or intervened before he was ready for her. He had to kill some time before he took Jalina to the final destination so he waited until after he got her to run his errand.

Pulling into the parking lot at Ace Hardware, Geoffrey was about to run out of patience. *Does this kid ever shut up?* She'd been blabbing on and on ever since she got in the car. He looked at her and she smiled up at him. "Wait here, okay? I gotta get a couple things. I'll be back in five minutes. In fact, you can time me and if I'm not back in time I'll buy you an ice cream. Deal?"

"Deal!" Jalina looked at her watch. "Okay, I'm ready. You can go in the store now."

Like I need your permission, you stupid brat. Geoffrey waved 'bye' as he headed into the store. He quickly grabbed a roll of duct tape and zip ties laughing to himself. *Hmm, what else goes in a kidnapper's tool kit?* He was confident he didn't need anything else. How hard could it be to contain an eleven-year-old kid?

When he got back to the car Jalina said, "Geoffrey, I'm hungry. When we get to the surprise can we have breakfast? I didn't get a chance to eat yet when you picked me up at Skyler's."

"Sure, kid," he said casually, not planning to feed her at all. She started jabbering away again telling him how much fun she'd had being Belle in the musical. He only feigned interest—he had much more sinister things on his mind.

Then she started singing, a song from that insufferable play he'd already had to sit through twice. That did it. He suddenly swerved off the road and made a hard right into a McDonald's drive-through. *Anything to shut this kid up. At least she can't sing while she's eating.*

"What do you want?" he waited.

"My mom says McDonald's is fast-food and fast-food is bad for you."

"Your mom is absolutely right. But just this one time it will be okay. It will be our little secret."

"But I don't like McDonald's food. It gives me a stomach ache."

"Have you ever had breakfast here?"

"No."

"Well, their breakfast food doesn't cause stomach aches. In fact, their hash browns are delicious."

"I like hash browns."

"Great." Then into the speaker he said, "Two orders of hash browns and two Egg McMuffins."

"May I have a water?"

"And two bottled waters."

When they got their food he tossed her the bags and told her she could eat now.

"Don't you want yours?"

"I'll wait until we get there."

He got on the freeway and called Tara for the third time. He got her voicemail—again. "Damn it."

"What's wrong, Geoffrey?"

"Huh? Oh, nothing."

"Is Mommy going to be there?" she asked, with a bite full of Egg McMuffin in her mouth, "When we get to the surprise?"

"Nope. It's just you and me. I thought we should spend some time together, get to know each other a little better. Don't you?"

"Oh yes!" she swallowed with an excited gulp, "Especially since you're going to marry my mom and become my stepdad!"

"Right." *Of course she told the kid, that bitch. Damn, who the hell didn't she tell? So much for asking her not to tell anyone.*

He drove on the freeway somewhat aimlessly until he finally got a hold of Tara. He needed the kid to be calm and in a good mood at this stage in the game. Tara finally picked up the fifth time he called.

Once he hung up it was time to put the rest of his plan into action. He drove through the parking lot of an abandoned building two blocks away from his office and parked on the side of the building. He'd passed by it many times and thought it might make a suitable hideout. It was once a small stationery and craft store but had gone out of business. Now it was empty.

Again, he asked Jalina to wait in the car. He grabbed his purchases and the duffle bag from the trunk then headed around to the back of the building. He smashed a window and let himself in.

He walked around inside and scoped the place out. It had been gutted. The inside was a dark, musty slab of concrete. The front windows were boarded up. It was perfect.

He went back out to the car. "Okay, Jalina. We're going to play a game. You like games, don't you?"

"Of course. Who doesn't?"

"Great. In this game I'm going to pretend to be a bad guy and you're going to pretend to be the princess who needs to be rescued."

"Oh, cool! Like an acting game?"

"Sure, yeah. But in this game, even though we're just acting, you have to do everything I tell you to, okay?"

"Okay."

"Good. Come on, let's go."

He led her to the back door he'd forced open and inside the store.

"It's so dark in here."

"I know."

"It's kind of scary."

"There's nothing to be scared of. It's just a little dusty is all."

"What if there's spiders?"

"If you see a spider just tell me and I'll kill it for you. Deal?"

"Deal."

Jalina cautiously explored the empty space as Geoffrey found an old folding table against the wall in what used to be an employee break room. He dragged it out, dusted it off, and set his bag on it.

He hopped up on the table in order to sit and eat his cold McDonald's breakfast. It tasted terrible by this point but he knew he'd need strength for what was to come. He forced down the congealed egg, rubbery ham, and cardboard-stiff English muffin. Then he took a few swigs of his water to wash it all down. *What a difference hot and fresh makes.*

"When does the game start?" Jalina asked.

"Soon. I'll let you know. For now, how about you walk through the entire building and report back to me what you find. Can you do that?"

"Sure, no problem." Jalina scampered off and Geoffrey began working on phase two of his plan.

34

Foot in Mouth

"JOE, I THINK you should sit down. There's a lot I haven't told you yet."

"Do you think sitting around chatting is going to help us find Jalina? Tara, we should be out there looking for her. We have to find our daughter. Where would he take her?"

"I don't know."

"That's it, I'm calling the police."

"No, don't. We should call Detective Reynolds."

"Who?"

"I told you. There's a lot you don't know. He called a few days ago to warn me that Geoffrey might be dangerous."

"You waited until now to tell me that? Is he wanted by the police?"

"When have I had the time? You just got back yesterday."

"Okay. Never mind. Can you call this Reynolds guy?"

"Yes, he gave me his number. Hold on…here it is."

"Call him!"

"I am!" Tara called Detective Reynolds while Joe paced. He answered on the first ring, "Reynolds."

"Detective, this is Tara Spencer. Geoffrey kidnapped my daughter and he won't tell me where he's taking her."

"When did you last have contact?"

"With Geoffrey? He called a couple minutes ago and told me he wants to spend the day with Jalina. He said he had a surprise planned and would let me know when he was ready for me."

"Are you home now?"

"Yes."

"Good. Stay there. Don't move and don't touch anything. If he calls, try to keep him on the phone as long as you can. I'll be right there." The call ended and Tara set her phone down.

"What did he say?" Joe's forehead veins were bulging from the stress.

"He said to stay here and he's on his way over."

Tara's phone rang. She snatched it up, "It's Geoffrey."

"Answer it."

"Geoffrey?"

"One more thing, *sweetie pie*. Don't call the cops. If you do, I'll know. If you do, the kid gets it." The line went dead.

"He said he'll kill Jalina if we call the cops. I have to call Detective Reynolds back. I have to tell him not to come."

Terror roared in her as she waited for Reynolds to answer his phone. No luck. It went straight to voicemail.

"It's too late. He's already on his way over here. Oh Joe, what are we going to do?" Tara sobbed.

"I think you better fill me in now."

Ten minutes later, someone pounded on the front door and Nala went nuts. Over the din of Nala's barking they heard a voice say, "Tara, it's Reynolds."

Tara hurried over, grabbed Nala's collar, and opened the door. She let in the detective and said, "After I talked to you, Geoffrey called and told me not to call the cops or he'll kill my daughter. I tried to call you back, to tell you not to come, but I got your voicemail."

"They all say that," Reynolds said as he stroked Nala's fur. She instantly settled down and licked his hand. "Don't worry about it. He's trying to scare you. He has no way of knowing who you've called."

"Okay, good. Thanks." Relieved, she released her grip on the dog and relaxed a little.

"Who's your friend?" Reynolds said, pointing to Joe.

"Hello Detective, I'm Joe Spencer, Jalina's father." Joe stepped forward and shook hands with Reynolds.

"Good. I'm glad you're both here and can work together on this."

"Meaning?" Joe asked.

"Meaning, many divorced couples can't stand to be in the same room with each other, much less be civil about it. I'm impressed with your maturity. Now, I have a few questions to ask Ms. Spencer if you don't mind."

"Not at all."

"Ms. Spencer, when was the last time you saw your daughter? I'm sorry, what is her name?"

"It's Jalina. I saw her last night at the cast party after her play. I drove her and a couple friends to the party then arranged for another mom to take them to Skyler's house to spend the night. Skyler is her best friend and they spend the night at each other's houses often."

"I see. Do you know for a fact that she stayed at Skyler's last night?"

"Yes. I went over there this morning at 9:30 to pick her up and Skyler's mom said Geoffrey had already picked her up at eight o'clock."

"What did he tell her?"

"Who?"

"What did Geoffrey say to Skyler's mom to get her to let Jalina leave with him?"

"Oh, sorry. It's hard to think clearly right now..."

"I understand. Take your time."

"He told Nicolee, Skyler's mom, that I asked him to pick up Jalina because I was at home cooking her favorite breakfast to surprise her."

"And Nicolee bought it?"

"Yes. Geoffrey can be pretty convincing."

Reynolds wrote something down in a notebook. "Ms. Spencer, would you mind showing me where Geoffrey spends most of his time? You mentioned a home office?"

"Yes, it's upstairs. I'll show you."

"Thank you."

Reynolds and Joe followed Tara upstairs to Geoffrey's office. She waited at the door and Reynolds walked in. "Is that his computer?"

"Yes, but it's password protected. I already tried to get in and couldn't."

"I'm sure the boys down at the lab can crack it. I'll radio in to have someone pick it up." Reynolds walked around the room searching for clues. He bent down and picked up a book off the floor, *Mindfulness-Based Cognitive Therapy.*

"That's for his practice. He's a therapist," Tara offered.

"Yes, I know. But anything could be a clue. Do you know why this book was on the floor?"

"No."

"I might. What was hanging over those two nails on the wall above the bookshelf? He could have knocked the book down when removing it."

Tara's eyes widened with terror as a stabbing feeling in her stomach reached all the way up to her throat.

"Ms. Spencer?"

"His katana," she barely whispered.

"Sorry, his what?" Reynolds snapped his fingers in front of Tara's face.

"He took his sword—a samurai sword! It's called a katana. Geoffrey is armed with a deadly weapon and he has Jalina. We have to find her before he hurts her. I'm afraid this is all my fault."

"Ms. Spencer, it's not your fault. Like you said, Geoffrey can be very convincing. He is a master manipulator and—" A knock on the door cut him off. "That'll be the boys from the lab. Don't touch anything. This room just became a crime scene. I'll let them in."

Five minutes later, Tara's condo swarmed with police officers and forensics experts. Joe and Tara were asked to sit on the couch, out of the way, until needed for questioning. The police officers set up upstairs in Geoffrey's office and declared it their Command Center.

Tara scrolled through the recent images on her digital camera, searching for one without stage makeup that she could give to the police. She'd taken so many pictures at the play she had to scroll a while until she found one that looked more like Jalina and less like Belle.

"Yoo hoo, anybody home?" Dorey's familiar voice wafted in from the front entry. "Hey, pretty lady, what's with the police cars outside? Who do I have to blow around here to make this whole thing go away, huh?"

Seeing Dorey put Tara over the edge. She broke down and sobbed in her hands.

"Was it something I said? Come on, that was a joke.

Don't cry. Tara? What's going on? Are you okay? For crying out loud, will someone please tell me who died?"

"Dorey, Jalina's been kidnapped. Geoffrey has her. The police are searching for clues that might tell them where he took her. They're breaking into his computer as we speak," Joe said in a monotone voice that defied emotion.

Joe and Dorey had met at a school event of Jalina's a few months back. She registered recognition and said, "Joe? What...Ohmygod, I am such an idiot," her hand shot up to her mouth. "Open mouth, insert foot...I didn't mean to be so crass. I shouldn't have said someone died... I'm so sorry...shit!"

"It's okay. You didn't know," Joe tried to smile at her. "And Jalina's not going to die. We're going to get her back. Everything is going to be fine. We will get her back." Joe's eyes flashed.

"Of course we will! What can I do?" Dorey met Joe's eyes, "Let's go get this mutherfucker!"

35

The Game

A POLICE SIREN wailed down the street and Geoffrey wondered if they were looking for him. *I told her not to call the cops. That bitch never listens to me.* If they searched for him at Dr. Nguyen's office, even though he hadn't been there in weeks, this place was too close for comfort. He chastised himself for not thinking of that.

"Okay, little missy, there's been a change of plans. Come on, we're going somewhere else."

Jalina happily got in the car because this place was dark and creepy. She didn't like this game. "Geoffrey, can we go home now? I miss my mom and I'm bored. You said the game would be fun but I'm not having fun anymore. Plus, I'm really tired."

"You can sleep in the car while I drive. Just tilt the seat back. We have to go one more place before we can go home, okay?"

"Okay…" she pouted but tilted the passenger seat back as far as she could so she could fall asleep.

Geoffrey drove to Huntington Beach and decided to go up to the rooftop of a five-story parking garage. It had a great vantage point and he figured he'd spot anyone coming before they got there. He'd be ready for them.

It was still daylight and Geoffrey didn't want to create a public spectacle so he decided to keep Jalina in the car for a while. No one else was on the roof. Not a soul. *Good thing it's January and not so touristy.* It was time to play the kidnapping game. He needed to be prepared.

"Okay Jalina, wake up. It's time to play the game now. I want you to stay in the car but I'm going to tie you up, okay? Remember, I'm pretending to be a bad guy and I just kidnapped the beautiful princess. Guess who the beautiful princess is?"

"Me?" she said huskily as she wiped the sleep from her eyes.

"That's right. You. This will be a terrific acting exercise. You'll make your mom so proud. Wait until you see the look on her face when she gets here. When I want you to act scared, I'll tell you, okay? Now, sit tight while I get the supplies."

"She's coming here? When? Are we putting on a show for her? Is that the surprise?"

"Yep, that's the surprise."

"Geoffrey, I'm hungry again. Are we gonna eat soon?"

"Of course. Right after your mom gets here. We'll put on the show for her and then we'll all go out for a nice dinner. Now stay right there. I'll be right back." *If I don't kill you to get you to stop talking first.*

He opened the trunk and rummaged through his bag. Taking out the zip ties he went back to the passenger side and bound Jalina's wrists and ankles with them. He had to be ready and in control when Tara got there.

He waited until sunset to make the call. He wanted to ensure the rooftop stayed deserted.

"Hello, Geoffrey? Where are you?" Tara demanded.

"Hello, Tara. We're ready for you, momma. Jalina and I have created a little show for you. Isn't that right, Jalina?"

"Hi Mommy. Geoffrey says you're gonna love our skit. It's called—"

"Uh uh, don't give it away just yet. We're at the Huntington Beach Parking Garage. The one on Main Street. Do you know the one I'm talking about?"

"Yes, I know it," Tara said.

"Come up to the rooftop. And, Tara?"

"What?"

"Come alone. If you don't, I'll know. I can see every car that enters the garage from here." He pushed the button and ended the call.

"Okay, princess. It's time to set the stage. Since your ankles are already bound I'm going to carry you to that light pole over there, okay?"

"Okay. I can't wait until Mommy sees our surprise show. Are we going to rehearse it? Or is it Improv?"

"Sure, let's have a run-through, shall we?" Geoffrey reached in the car and picked up Jalina. He carried her over to the light pole in the middle of the roof. He set her down on the ground in front of it and thought of something else.

"Now I have to tie you to the light pole to make sure you don't get away. Stay right there, I have to get the rope." He jogged back to the car, realized he didn't have any rope, and grabbed the duct tape.

While at the car he took his katana out of the duffel bag and slid it into the holster on his back, which was already carefully in place under his shirt. He slammed the trunk shut and jogged back over to Jalina. He wound the tape a few times around her chest and the pole. *This kid's not going anywhere.*

"That's not rope, silly."

"You're right, it's not. But we don't have any rope so we have to improvise…. There, that ought to hold you for a while."

"But just for pretend, right?"

"Right. Of course, silly. But we have to make it look real so your mom can see what a good actress you are, right?"

"Right," Jalina smiled, but it was starting to feel a little too real.

"Hmm, what shall we do until your mom gets here? Oh, I know. Do you want to hear a story?"

"Sure," Jalina relaxed a little.

"Once upon a time, there was a very handsome man."

Jalina giggled. "Is that you?"

"Shhh, don't interrupt," he cleared his throat. "Once upon a time, there was a very handsome man. The handsome man was married to a beautiful lady, but the lady had three very unruly children."

"Were those your stepchildren?"

"I thought I told you not to interrupt me," he glared at her. "That's it. I've been waiting all day to do this."

Geoffrey grabbed the roll of duct tape, tore a strip off and put it over Jalina's mouth. "There. Now I can finish my story in peace. Let's see…where was I?" He scratched his chin and looked at her.

"You want to know something, Jalina? I've never been a kid person. Truth is, I can't stand kids. Funny, huh? Yet I keep falling for women with kids. What's that all about? My last wife had three, as I was trying to tell you when you so rudely interrupted me. Twin girls and an obnoxious spoiled brat son who called the cops on me every time he felt threatened.

"That was two years ago." Geoffrey began pacing back and forth in front of her. "My life was a lot different then. I had a big house and made a lot of money. My wife was a total knock out. Hell, she should be. I paid enough money for all those plastic surgeries. Fake nose, fake boobs, fake life. She was a whiny little bitch; nothing was ever good enough for her."

Geoffrey began to revel in the sound of his own voice as it boomed on the rooftop. No longer playing the game, no longer thinking of Jalina, he meandered all over the rooftop. He delighted in telling his story and continued, without even looking at his captive audience. *She's captive, that's for sure.*

"I suppose I had a bit of a mid-life crisis when I hit forty-two. But I turned it into a cathartic experience and purged everything from my life that didn't make me happy. That included, well…" he laughed. "Everything. I walked away from my wife, her kids, my job, my house—all of it. Gone. Poof," he snapped his fingers.

"The bitch trapped me. The kids' dad was a real piece of work too; total deadbeat. I kicked his ass and told him to stay the hell away from them. He tried to sue me, too—*me*. Whatever. The fucking prick. He got what he deserved. So, the little wifey trapped me into playing the daddy role—which I hated. And I hated her for it even more."

As if suddenly remembering Jalina was there, he spun around and stared at her. There she was, the guest of honor; the most important person in Tara's life. *I warned her not to put her kid before me.*

He sauntered over to the light pole and knelt down in front of Jalina. "And then I met your mom. A real class act, that one. But so gullible. Man, I could get her to do anything I wanted," he sneered.

"Except when it came to you. Jalina this and Jalina that. Ugh. I got so sick of hearing your name, of hearing her sing your praises. And I'll never sit through another one of your boring plays or stupid concerts ever again. You can be sure of that, kid.

"She loves you more than she ever loved me. She won't even move out of that dump of hers because she doesn't want you to have to change schools. Oh, poor little Jalina can't leave her friends. And now she thinks she can just get rid of me? Toss me out with the trash?"

Jalina's eyes grew wide. "Oh yeah, you didn't know about that did you?"

She shook her head.

"Yep, she kicked me out last night. Told me to get out. She thinks I'm yesterday's news. Well, I've got news for both of you—she's gonna pay." Geoffrey stopped and looked at her. "It's inspection time. Mommy will be here soon."

He examined the zip ties around her wrists and ankles and tightened them with glee. A single tear escaped her eye and rolled down her cheek, her pupils dilated.

"Oh, come on. You can do better than that. It's time for your Academy award-winning performance, sweetheart. Where's the terror?" He leaned in close and whispered in her ear, "This is the part where you need to be scared now. You see, after I slowly torture you in front of your groveling mommy...I'm going to kill you both."

He reached a hand out to Jalina's face and she jerked her head back. He laughed.

"So, you've got a little fight in you? That's good. This will be fun."

He caressed her cheek and wiped a tear away with his thumb. Then he grabbed the tape that was across her mouth and ripped it off in one sudden motion.

Out of her mouth came the high pitched, raw scream of a child in pain. *Music to my ears.*

"There, that's better. Very convincing. Why, Jalina, you're a very good little actress." He tilted his head back and laughed maniacally.

"I don't want to play this game anymore," Jalina said in a surprisingly strong voice.

"But it's just starting to get fun. Aren't you having fun? I sure am."

Car tires squealed on the pavement below. Geoffrey looked at the ramp and saw headlights coming toward them.

"It's showtime. Here comes Mommy."

36

Endgame

JOE INSISTED ON driving to the parking garage even though Tara wasn't sure it was a good idea.

"Geoffrey said I had to come alone," she objected.

"Tara, there's no way I'm letting you walk into that trap alone," he urged. "We're getting our daughter and we're getting her together. Got it?"

"Got it," Tara agreed.

Detective Reynolds told them to wait for back up. He said to sit tight and they would come up with an airtight plan to get Jalina back safely. While Reynolds was devising a plan of attack with his team, Joe and Tara enlisted Dorey's help to create a diversion.

Dorey got up from her chair and strolled over to where the policeman was standing. She stretched and yawned and bumped into him, causing him to spill his coffee on his uniform, shoes, and the floor.

"Oh, I'm so sorry! Please forgive me, Officer…?"

"McClaine, ma'am."

"Officer McClaine, I'm so clumsy. Here, let me help you wipe that up," she wiped at his trousers with her hands.

"That's okay, I got it. Maybe you could get me a towel?" Officer McClaine said.

"Of course, there's one right here in the kitchen. I'll show you." Dorey put her hand on his upper arm to turn him around and steer him toward the kitchen. As he turned she flicked her eyes to Tara to signal them to sneak out. "Oh my, what big biceps you have," she fluttered her eyelashes and giggled.

Tara rolled her eyes but wasted no time in tiptoeing with Joe to the front door. They heard more giggles as they eased the door closed behind them and ran to Joe's car.

"Remind me to kiss Dorey when this is all over," Joe said. "I'll be damned if I'm going to sit around a second longer while that maniac has our daughter."

Driving up and around the never-ending ramp to the top of the parking garage, Joe and Tara heard a scream that sent a shot of adrenaline and terror coursing through them. Joe stepped on the gas harder before his brain registered why. "Oh my god, was that Jalina?"

Nearing the top they could see Jalina tied up to the light pole. Before waiting for the car to stop Tara's door flew open and she jumped out, feet hitting the pavement at a run. She ran straight for her child, ignoring the plan she and Joe had just come up with in the car.

Her legs pounded furiously on the pavement, heart thudding in her ears. *Breathe. Calm. Breathe. Mindful. I can't help her if I'm hysterical. Think.*

"Hello, Tara. It's so good to see you. Where do you think you're off to in such a hurry?" Geoffrey caught up with her, blocking her path. "Aren't you going to give me a kiss? Where are your manners?" He grabbed her and tried to kiss her. Joe snuck up behind him and hit him on the temple with his cell phone.

"What's this?" Geoffrey turned around and saw Joe, bloody cell phone in hand. He wiped his temple and licked the blood from his fingers, tasting the metallic tang. "You think you can take me down with a cell phone?" he laughed.

Turning his back on Joe he pursued Tara again. "Tsk, tsk, Tara," he called out after her. "You've been a bad girl. I told you to come alone, didn't I?" he nearly caught up to her. "You never listen. Jalina and I have a show to perform for you. I was about to put the finishing touches on it when you two sho—"

"Over my dead body," Joe seethed. He kicked Geoffrey between his legs from behind, but not quite attaining his intended target.

Geoffrey turned on him. "I can arrange that," he growled. He aimed for Joe's nose and connected. Blood spattered on Joe's shirt.

Joe staggered back, blood cascading from his nose. But he remained determined. He knew what he had to do.

He took a deep, steadying breath and hurtled himself at Geoffrey.

Joe's head rammed into Geoffrey's stomach, knocking the wind out of him and causing Geoffrey to lose his balance.

As the two men fell to the ground Joe yelled, "RUN!" at a wide-eyed Tara.

She watched them scuffle and roll around on the ground, like some bizarre wrestling match. Her legs felt weighted down and she couldn't move.

Suddenly, as if a switch had flipped on, Tara sprang into

action.

She ran to Jalina, "I'm here, baby. We're gonna be okay." She broke through the duct tape around Jalina's chest with her teeth.

The tape was thicker than she thought. *How many times did he wrap this around her? There are too many layers.*

In a panicked frenzy, she gnawed at the tape like a rat gnawing through a wooden trap.

"Mommy hurry! Please!" Jalina cried, tears streaming down her face.

Finally freeing her from the pole, Tara quickly examined her daughter and took in the puffy red face wet with tears, the terror in her eyes. But thankfully she seemed uninjured. Tara hoisted her daughter up over her shoulder and ran toward Joe's car.

The keys! She stopped in her tracks.

Joe's car keys were in his pocket. At the moment, he was a little too busy to toss them to her.

Think. Think. Thin—the stairs!

With Jalina still over her shoulder, Tara ran to the top of the stairs. Once there, she put Jalina down.

She shimmied open the zip ties by inserting her thumbnail into the lock.

She freed Jalina's wrists.

She did the same thing with the zip ties around her ankles. Once they were off, she held Jalina by the shoulders and looked in her eyes.

"Are you okay? Can you run?"

"Yes, Mommy. I can run."

But it was too late. Geoffrey grabbed Tara and spun her around.

"Where do you think you're going?" he taunted, one eye swollen and half closed, blood dripping down his face.

"Stay away from my daughter, asshole." Tara punched

Geoffrey in the throat. She shook her hand and rubbed it, realizing she'd dug her fingernails into her palm and it was bleeding.

He choked and sputtered as he leaned back. His hands grasped at his throat and he stood precariously close to the edge of the stairwell. He tried to get his breath back.

"I should push you down the stairs," Tara spat.

"Do it," he choked out. "I dare you."

"I'm not a murderer—like you."

Detective Reynolds appeared at the top of the stairs and grabbed Geoffrey from behind. Reynolds had him in handcuffs before he could fight back.

"Well, if it isn't my old nemesis: Jeff the wife-beater. I've been waiting for you to do something stupid. Now I finally get to take you away where you belong. Let's go over here and have a little chat, shall we?"

"Reynolds," Geoffrey hissed.

"Ms. Spencer, are you and the girl okay?" Detective Reynolds asked.

"Yes, sir. We're okay," Tara held onto Jalina as she clung to her mom. "Thank goodness, you got here just in time."

"Perhaps. But you should have waited for me," Reynolds sighed.

Tara looked over at Geoffrey with loathing, "Looks like you're going to rot in prison after all, Geoffrey."

Detective Reynolds shoved and manhandled Geoffrey across the parking lot, closer to the light pole. He wanted him under the light where he could keep an eye on him.

Tara and Jalina started to follow but Tara saw an unconscious Joe lying on the ground by Geoffrey's car. She ran over to him.

"Detective Reynolds? Joe's badly hurt. Can you help him?"

Reynolds turned to answer her. "I've already radioed

back up and an ambulance. Help is on the way. Is he breathing?"

She reached down to check Joe's pulse, her heart racing with fear. *There's so much blood.*

She wiped at the blood under his jaw and put two fingers to his pulse.

It was beating, if faintly. *Thank you, God.*

"Yes, he has a pulse."

"Good. Hang tight. The ambulance should arrive any minute now. I just need to deal with Jensen here so we can lock him up properly," Reynolds said and turned back toward Geoffrey.

"Never," Geoffrey hissed.

He snapped the handcuffs apart.

Still holstered under his shirt was the katana.

He drew it.

Reynolds reached for his gun. The white of his throat gleamed under the fluorescent glow of the light pole.

The flash of the katana shimmered as it sliced through Reynolds' throat in one fluid movement…as though it had performed that maneuver a hundred times in some ancient battlefield.

Reynolds crumpled at Geoffrey's feet—dead before he hit the ground.

"Mommy! Look out!" Jalina screamed, still standing by her dad's listless body.

Tara spun around and stood up as Geoffrey charged toward her, brandishing his katana.

Her hands covered in Joe's blood, she kicked Geoffrey with all her strength between the ribs. A quiet rage boiled to the surface for every wrong he had committed against her and those she loved. The lies. The mind games. Nala. Dorey. Her faith. Joe. *Her daughter!*

He staggered back and dropped the katana. It skidded

across the asphalt with a grating sound.

She ran at him and kicked him again.

Between the legs.

She felt stronger than she ever had. She felt a surge of power and knew this man would never hurt her again.

He screamed out and doubled over—his face a contorted ball of pain.

He tripped backwards over his feet.

Geoffrey fell hard, landing with a thud inches from the edge.

He curled up into the fetal position—moaning.

He looked up at Tara as she contemplated what to do next. She could feel the adrenaline still coursing through her veins as she stood over him.

"It's over, Geoffrey. Just stay there 'til the police get here and no one else needs to get hurt, okay?"

Their eyes met.

"I'm going to kill you, you fucking bitch. And for good measure, I'm going to kill your precious little girl, too," he wheezed.

His eyes flicked to the katana twelve feet away as he started to push himself up.

"Wrong answer. I told you to stay away from my daughter."

With one final kick, Tara sent him over the edge.

She watched as Geoffrey Jensen fell to his death.

"You never listen," she said.

Jalina ran to her mom. They wrapped their arms around each other and clung to one another, sobbing.

"Mommy, I was so scared. I thought he was going to kill you."

"Not a chance. I'm here, baby. I'm not going anywhere. I love you so much."

"I love you too, Mommy. Is Daddy going to be okay?"

"I hope so, sweetie. I hope so."

An ambulance and two police cars careened up the ramp, sirens wailing. The paramedics loaded Joe, still unconscious, into the ambulance and rushed him to the hospital.

Officer McClaine, the policeman Dorey had flirted with back at the house, told Tara he'd drive her and her daughter to see Joe as soon as they answered a few more questions.

"Oh, and Ms. Spencer?"

"Yes?"

"That little bait and switch stunt you and your ex-husband pulled at the house with your friend? I saw right through that."

"Did you?"

"Yes. You're lucky I have a fondness for red heads."

"Is that so?"

"Indeed. It turns out Miss Dalton and I have a lot in common. In fact, I've scheduled an appointment with her to inquire further."

"An appointment?"

"Well, some might call it a date," he winked at her. "We'll be seeing each other again in a more casual setting."

"I see." *Way to go Dorey.*

37

Family

TARA AND JALINA visited Joe in the hospital. He had a broken nose, a punctured lung, and two fractured ribs. But the doctor assured Tara he'd make a full recovery.

"How do I look?" Joe asked.

"Like you were beaten up by a psychopath," Tara replied.

"Funny, that's exactly how I feel." They laughed.

Joe winced, "Ouch, guess I better tone it down on the laughter for a few days. Jalina, you are not allowed to make me laugh, do you understand?"

"I understand, Daddy," she giggled. "I won't make you laugh, I promise. I wouldn't want to hurt you. But is it okay if I hug you?"

"Gently."

Jalina rested her hands on her dad's shoulders and leaned down to put her cheek on his chest. She stayed there a minute and listened to his heartbeat.

"I love you, Daddy."

"I love you too, Squirt."

"Mom, may I get a snack out of the vending machine in the hall? I'm hungry."

"Of course, honey. It's been a very long day. I think we're all hungry." She pulled a five dollar bill out of her purse. "Here you go, sweetie. I'll be right there."

"Okay, thanks."

Joe and Tara watched silently as Jalina walked out of his hospital room and down the hall. He turned to Tara and asked, "How did we raise such a good kid?"

"I don't know. Just lucky, I guess."

"Tara, I owe you an apology."

"For what? For trying to warn me I was engaged to a psycho?"

"Ha ha. Ouch," he grimaced. "Yeah, something like that."

"I forgive you. I know you only want what's best for us. Friends?"

"No, not friends," Joe said.

Tara frowned.

"Family."

"Family," she agreed. She gazed at him a moment, relieved that he'd be okay. She was relieved that they'd all be okay—especially Jalina. She thought of what could have happened, what almost happened. *No.* She shook her head. She couldn't let her mind go there. She never wanted to think about this terrible day again.

"You should get some rest," she finally said. "It's been a long day. We'll come back in the morning." She squeezed Joe's hand then turned and walked toward the door.

"Tara?"

"Yes?"

"I'll always love you, ya know. You're the mother of my child."

"I'll always love you too, Joe."

Tara smiled at Joe and walked out of the hospital room.

ACKNOWLEDGMENTS

I owe a big thank you to my editor and cheerleader, Tamara Anne Fowler. Thank you for finding the words I meant to use and for corralling and reigning in my over abundant use of commas. I'm sure my readers will thank you too.

To Kristi Shimada, thank you for encouraging me from day one. Your belief in me helped drive me to finish this book, when I just wanted to procrastinate and binge watch a few *Friends* reruns instead. I also deeply appreciate your knowledge and insights of the Japanese Internment Camps and Japanese-American culture during World War II.

Special thanks to Jason Brick, author friend and Martial Arts expert, for teaching me how to fight. Or, at least how to write a plausible fight scene.

I also want to thank RE Vance, my book coach, for helping me develop my seedling of an idea into something readable. You amaze me with your ability to pick up on a thread of an idea and help weave it into a full story. You're also adept at offering encouragement and advice to keep me focused on what's important—writing.

I am indebted to my early readers and writing community. A special shout out to Tiana, Julie, Emily, Nola, Karley, and Brandi. Your constructive feedback, support, and eagle eye at catching those dreaded typos is most appreciated. Writing seems like a solo task, but it takes a village. Thank you for being my village.

A very special thank you goes to Glenn Madrid, for giving me permission to use his beloved wife Dorey's name and essence as my favorite character in this book. She left this world too soon and we all miss her immensely. Dorey was a devoted wife, mother, teacher, and friend to all who knew her. Sadly, she lost her battle with breast cancer July 15, 2018. I can picture her now, pen at the ready, poised to write all over the margins of this book to tell me what I got wrong—and what I got right.

My biggest thank yous go to my mom and my daughter —my two favorite people on the planet. You were my first readers and are my biggest fans. You believed in me when no one else did. You supported me to reach for the stars and follow my dreams. I love you forever and always.

And finally, to you, the reader. Thank you for taking a chance on an unknown writer. I hope you enjoyed Tara's story.

About the Author

Tasche Laine is the author of the 2018 International Book Award winning *Closure: based on a true story* and *Chameleon*, the sequel to *Closure*. She is the proud mom of a college student and currently resides in the Pacific Northwest. For more information, please visit her website at taschelaine.com or follow her on Facebook.com/TascheLaine.

A note from the author…
Thank you for reading *Chameleon*. If you enjoyed it and would like to know when new releases come out, please join my mailing list for updates on future books and other writing projects, at taschelaine.com.

If you enjoyed this book, I'd like to ask you for a favor. Will you please post an honest review for *Chameleon* on Amazon and Goodreads? A review is the best gift you could give an author.

To see how it all began, read *CLOSURE*. It's Tara's slice of life tale about love and loss, and her journey to reconnect with her first love. It is available online and in book stores.

Made in the USA
Columbia, SC
16 March 2019